" The BOOK "

of

" Strange Facts and Calculations "

Written by

Joseph Willis

Pseudonym: Will James

Started in the Year 1998

" Note "

I was taught the Math in " The BOOK " by a person who was
very effulgent in Mathematics and Engineering
and is older than " Time " itself.

His name is: 3.14159265 to the 10th power divide by 47171060.81

" Note "

All the " Information " in this "Book" is based on, Facts, Fiction,
Non-Fiction, True Facts And None at All.

" THE PAPER "
STRANGE FACTS AND CALCULATIONS

Author: Mr. Will James

Copyright ©2010

Written by:

Mr. Will James

Printed in the United States of America

Published April 1, 2021

ISBN: 978-0-578-83196-1

ISBN: 13 - 978-0-578-83196-1

Contact Information:

AuthorWillJames@gmail.com

DPD PUBLISHING
Dr. Patricia Demps

www.DrPatriciaD.com

PUBLISHING PROPERTY OF:

Dr. Patricia Demps

AuthorPatriciaD@gmail.com

www.DrPatriciaD.com

"STRANGE FACTS AND CALCULATIONS"

My Book *"Strange Facts and Calculations"* is the compilation of many stories, facts, fiction and nonfiction. It is several paper's that make up the most interesting tells based on true and non-true events, characters and destinations to be determined as Truth or Non Truth by its readers. My Stories follow world and non-world events. Dates, time and characters that appear to be real and can be, but may or may not be; the reader must decide if it is too real to be true, or if it is indeed Fact, Fiction or if they even care, because they are enjoying it either way.

It is distinguished from other titles very simply by its seen and unseen message in the title. The Title states that it is *Strange Facts And Calculations*; but as the reader starts to read, he or she will have to decide. Many of the Readers will be Wow'd by what appears to be Fiction, while others will know that they are facts and think: Hmmmmm, I Never even thought about that. Others will be amazed and dazzled by the Calculations, and many more will be pleased to have picked up a novel of such *"Strange Facts And Calculations"* and for it to be so real, true, but yet, wondering and guessing, "is it really true?" This depth and creativity not only distinguishes this, The Paper *"Strange Facts And Calculations"*, from other titles, but it is exactly what it states in the title…..Strange Strange Facts, and Many Many Calculations.

I am Who I am and most qualified in deed. I am qualified to write such papers and compile them into such a compilation not only because I have lived most of the pages I have written; I have been personally involved, or have seen, read or witnessed the subjects at hand, (before, after or during such an ordeal), but they were and are *"Strange Facts And Calculations"*.

As witnessed by myself and others, some of the most unique events in the History of the World, The United States of America, The State of Texas and the City of Dallas (among other Countries, Cities and States). Strange Not only to me, but I have put them in writing, calculated them, ask others their thoughts on events and presented facts, and calculations as well as mentioned strange facts to get a response or reaction (and I have ask these questions, or presented the facts and my calculations to many people from different age groups, genres, genders and social status). I am qualified to write this book because I was/am alive and can share these stories vocally, and descriptively with anyone and everyone who wishes to hear and listen. I am open and ready to share with the inquisitive minds that yearn to hear and read "Strange Facts", Fiction and Nonfiction. I am qualified to write of these events because I have calculated most of them myself; like the death of the 7 Astronauts when the space shuttle Columbia Blew up Over Dallas Texas, Feb 1, 2003. It's a strange factual relation to relevant events in History. Such as its calculation to the Death on the date of November 22, 1963 on a street in Dallas, Texas 3 months, and 40 years earlier….both in a year ending in the number 3, and I "Mr. Will James" being a Witness to both unnerving and deathly shattering events. Not only this Strange Fact, My calculations, revelations and notes, but indeed these Facts qualify me to write this book.

I know my book will sell. My book says what many people have thought, think, or want to hear. Many more are curious, nosy, or are not sure, but because it is a possibility they have a desired interest that beats within and pushes one to go out and purchase, then have a conversation with others that then need their own copy to see, read, agree with, disagree with, calculate on their own, or propose their words or thoughts to it and/or Relevant events in their own lives, or simply state how they see or saw such events. While many others will be prompted to ask…..If any of it is true at all, or if None, all will be intrigued, and relieved that it was put into print and feel as if it was said out loud. Inquiring Minds Always Want to Know.

The subjects on these papers, parallel with life events, actual events and the lives of so many others that may, and must share and tell a friend as well debate and carry on such a conversation to generate just enough curiosity to get those that know to talk; The Media.

These papers speak of the times, challenges, and events that many have pushed to the side, want to hear, wish they could, or would have said and yet leave many guessing and Wondering: …..Is this True???

The Paper "*Strange Facts and Calculations*" is what pulls and pushes at the heart and soul of People in General. Readers of a Certain Genre, Culture, Politicians, Educated Men, Women, Teens, and Young Adults. The Curious by Nature and those that see it and say: Hmmmmm. This Book will intrigue Everyday People, the Housewife, the Pastor, the deaconess and the lady of the night.

My Novel Dares to state, say, and tell the Stories through my Eye's with the assured sentiment that Truth bears witness to all, or it is simply a Great Read of what could be, is, or was "*Strange Facts and Calculations*".

The Burning questions make for a Great Sell, Book Signings, Readings and Questions answered. The Ready will Beg for more, and I have been alive long enough, have seen, can envision just enough to make it a series of compilations with many more; Questions, Answers and a perspective on what many want to say, know, or are just nosy enough to want to see, hear and listen to.

You ask me to tell you Why I believe My Book Will Sell? I have just given you minimal Reasons of Why I Know it Will Sell. It has shock Value. My Title is Distinguished from other Titles and inspires curiosity at first Glance (as the Cover will enhance).

The first 2/3 pages will get the reader, and for those that like to run to the back, it will have them at first glance. I am Qualified to write this book as I am the Author of each paper of the compilation, and it sells itself. I am who I am, and This Book was written to market and Sell.

I am, Mr. Will James.

*Witnessed by Dr. Patricia Demps.

THE   PAPER

AUTHOR'S   NOTE

The Stories in this book are based on true life Stories and True Events. I have tried to write each story as close as I could, just like it happened. The names in these stories are Fictional.

Will James

Congratulations

Mr. Will James

You have Successfully completed

Psychic & Intuitive Development

and are awarded this diploma in recognition of your accomplishments.

For the Sept 2008 - Sept 2009 Class of Psychic and Intuitive Development Meetup group in Forney, Texas.

_____September 10, 2009_____

Prophetess, Dr. Patricia Demps

INTRODUCTION

You may wonder just how " The Paper " came into being. It all started in 1998, as I was going to water School to get my state water License. I had to learn a lot of water calculations and got to wondering how to calculate some things that I was told in school that could not be done.

Some of the things that I calculated in " The Paper " was the size of the " Universe ", How Old the earth is and one that became more famous than Mr. Einstein's little equation "E = mc2 ", The calculations of the Speed of Sun Light. While working some water calculations, I found a number 177245.385 and for some unknown reason compared it to the speed of light which is 186,300.000; using Mr. Einstein's little equation " E = mc2 ", I squared 177245.385 and it became " Pi " to the 10th power.

I wrote a page of a very large calculation and a friend at work put it on the internet. It was read by a female Professor at the University of Texas in Austin, Texas that was teaching Calculus and she and her class were blown away by it. She sent my friend an Email telling him how amazed she was at the paper. I then gave it the name " The Paper ". And after working on the calculation in it, I got to wondering how strange it was that I could work and understand some very large calculations that no one else could. I could not understand the small numbers in the game of " Dominos ", and some other strange Facts about my Life also came to light. I then added " Strange Facts and Calculations " to the name " The Paper ".

When you first start to read "The Paper " and get through the math pages in it, you will get to some pages that you may think are " Science Fiction " but are real and true Facts about me, and some people in my life. I tried to write everything down just like it happened. There is one page in " The Paper " that will prove to the Reader that what they are reading is not " Fiction "; but I will not tell you which page it is here. Each page in " The Paper " has a Title and you will need to reach the Title of each and every page first to understand as best you can, each page you read.

" Note To The Reader "

 Some pages in " The Paper ", which I later changed to " The Book ", are sensitive reading. NO harm was intended to any reader. After reading all of my " Paper ", you may wonder just " Who " I am?

I am " Nobody Really ". Just a man that somehow has a very " Strange Gift ".

The Ability To Walk Through Time and Change The Future.

Will James …………

THE BOOK

INDEX

Page Number:

THE PAPER

THE PAPER

" The True Speed of Light "

.

There are two ways to measure the "Speed of Light". The First = is by Mechanical means which was done by the use of a laser beam. This speed was determined to be 186,300.000 miles per second. The Second = is by Mathematics. This is the "True Speed of Light" as determined by Math. This speed is 177,245.385 miles per second. A difference of 9,054.615 miles per second. This makes the speed of light by Math slower not faster than the Mechanical measurement of the speed of light. As Mr. Einstein did not know of the Mathematical measurement of the speed of light when he wrote the equation $E = mc2$. Therefore, his calculation was wrong when he worked the equation " $E = mc2$ ".

The Mechanical measurement of the speed of light is a Negative number and is not relative to any part of the Calculation which causes the Calculation to fall short of its full Potential. $E = mc2$ is the Mathematical measurement of Time, Light and Space. By using the Mathematical speed of light in the equation and squaring it, it becomes "Pi", thus giving a continuance to the equation and making the Mathematical measurement a Positive number.

In page 11 of " The Paper ", I proved what I said here.

.

.

.

.

" Note "

.

.

.

. 186,300.000 m/s x 60 x 60 x 24 x 365 = 5.8751568 to the 12th power miles in 1 light year by the Mechanical Measurement.

. 177245.385 m/s x 60 x 60 x 24 x 365 = 5.589610461 to the 12th power miles in 1 light year by the Mathematical Measurement. A difference of 2.85546339 to the 11th power in miles in the 2 light years.

.

.

.

By: Will James

THE PAPER

" The Mathematical Speed of Light is 177245.385 miles per second "

.   177245.385 squared will = 3.14159265 to the 10th divide by the year 5792 B.C. will = 5,425,020.46. If you add this number together 5, 4, 2, 5, 0, 2, 0, 4, 6 it will = 27. Divide 3.14159265 to the 10th by 27 it will   = 1,163,552,833 x 4803.916335 will = 5.589610461 to the 12th which is 1 light year by the Mathematical speed of Light. Now take 5,424,020.46 divided by 27 it will = 200,889.6467. Divide 3.14159265 to the 10th by 200,889.6467 will = 156,384.

Now add up 1, 5, 6, 3, 8, 4 it will = 27.

If you take the year 5792 B.C. x 27 it will = 156,384 or 27. 27 is the number used to multiply square feet to get square yards. Now again you can see why 186,000 miles per second is only a number and not the True Speed of Light.

By: Will James

2

THE PAPER

" Time Travel "
The Age of the Earth

Science has placed the age of the Earth at or about 150,000,000 years old. The " Bible " has placed it at or about 7,000 years old. The bible's 7,000 years old is 5,000 years B.C. and 2,000 years A.D. for a total of 7,000 years old. Page 3 of " The Paper " will show that both are right and that Mr. Einstein's theory of " Time Travel " is more Reality than Theory. Through the use of the " Mathematical Measurement of the Speed of Light," I will show how the Earth Aged both by " Science " and " The Bible " because of the reality of " Time Travel ". One light year by Mathematics is 5.589610461 to the 12th power x 7,000 years = 3.912727323 to the 16th power in light years. The Earth being 25,000 miles around at the Equator, will travel 25,000 miles in one revolution which takes 24 hrs. 24 hours equal's 1 day. So 25,000 miles x 365 days will equal 9,125,000 miles traveled in one year x 7,000 years will = 6.3875 to the 10th power miles traveled in the " Bible's " 7,000 years in Rotation. Now take the 3.91272323 to the 16th power in light years by Mathematics in the " Bible's " 7,000 years and divide it by 6.3875 to the 10th power in miles of rotation in 7,000 years and it will equal 612,559.4098 miles x 365 days in a year and it will equal 223,584,184.6 years old.

" The True Age of the Earth as We Know it by Mathematics."

By: Will James

THE PAPER

" E = mc2 "

In the equation $E = mc2$, E being Energy is the one thing giving Substance to Matter and Matter being the bases for Light. Light then becomes the end Product of Energy, thus Creating a Circle. " Time Travel " is like a clock, it can only move in a Circle and not in a Straight Line. So with the Rotation of the Earth, Light travels through the Earth's Magnetic Fields, thus Creating a Natural Phenomenon that is " Time Travel ". On the other hand, if " Time Travel " was to encounter a " Black Hole " in Space, it would travel in a Straight Line due to the fact that there is no Matter in a " Black Hole ", and Matter is what Creates a Circle in the Universe. To better put it, in Layman's Language a " Black Hole " is where " Reality Stops " and " Nothing Begins ".

By: Will James

THE PAPER
" How to Figure the " Size of the Universe "

The Universe was built and based on Mathematics. The key to all of it is 177245.385.

This Number represents the " Mathematical Speed of Light." This number with in itself can measure the Size of the " Universe and Everything in It." To measure the Size of The Universe, you must first determine its " Diameter ", as it is based on the Circle. To find this, you have to use the number for the " Mathematical Speed of Sun Light ", (note : found in page 11) of 1.77245385 to the 11th m/s x 60 will = 1.06347231 to the 13th x 60 will = 6.38083386 to the 14th m/h x 24 will = 1.531400126 to the 16th m/d x 31.536 days/ month will = 4.829423439 to the 17th m/m x 12 m/y will = 5.795308126 to the 18th miles/ sun light year x 863,190 the Diameter of the Sun in miles will = 5.002452021 to the 24 power in Sunlight years, the " Diameter of the Universe ".

.   To figure the " Volume of the Universe ", you have to use the equation for Volume which is Pi x r2 . First set up the equation as shown   =

.

Pi   x   R   x   R

. Now divide the Diameter of the Universe which is 5.002452021 to the 24 power in Sun Light Years by 2 and it will = 2.501226011 to the 24 power which is the " Radius ".
. Now to find " Pi " for this equation use the equation E = mc2 and take the number for the " Mathematical Speed of Sun Light " 1.77245385 to the 11th which is (c) in the equation and square it. It will be 3.14159265 to the 22 power which is " Pi " to the 22 power.

.   Now put this number under " Pi " in the equation as shown.
.

Pi   r   r

. 3.14159265 to the 22 power   x   2.501226011 to the 24 power   x   2.501226011 to the 24 power will = 1.965421692 to the 69 power the Volume of The Universe in " Sun Light Years.
.
.

To find the " Diameter " of All Creation, take the Volume of the " Universe " and Square it.   1.965421692 to the 69 power squared will $=$ E o . The " Diameter of all Creation ".

.

.

.

By: Will James

THE PAPER

" The Universe is Really Big "

.

1.77245385 to the 11th power in miles per second is the " Mathematical Speed of Sun Light ".

. That equals 1.06347231 to the 13th power in miles per min. x 60 = 6.38083386 to the 14th power in miles per hour x 24 = 1.531400126 to the 16th power in miles per day x 31.536 days per month will = 4.829423439 to the 17th power in miles per month x 12 months per year = 5.795308126 to the 18th power in miles in 1 Sun Light Year.

. 1.965421692 to the 69th power in Sun Light Years is the Volume of the Universe. Take 1.965421692 to the 69th power in Sun Light Years and divide it by 6.38083386 to the 14th power in miles per hour and it will = 3.080195685 to the 54th power in hours. There is 8,760 hours in the Earth Year. Now divide 3.080195685 to the 54th power in hours by 8,760 hours and it will = 3.516205119 to the 50th power in Earth years. Now divide 3.516205119 to the 50th power in Earth Years by 70 years in an average life time and it will = 5.023150171 to the 48th power in lift times to travel the full size of the " Universe " at a Speed of 6.38083386 to the 14th power in miles per hour.

Now I hope you can understand why "Aliens" are not seen in Outer Space. As it is due to the Speed needed to cross the " Universe ".

By: Will James

THE PAPER

" 6 6 6 The Angel of Light "

.
.
.
.
.   The Earth travels at a speed of 66,600 miles per hour around the Sun. The Mathematical Speed of Light 177245.385 divided by 66,600 = 2.661342117.

.Now divide 177245.385 by 6 6 6 the Mark of " The Beast "   it will = 266.1342117.

.This will help you to understand how the Universe was Based on Mathematics.

.
.
.

By: Will James

THE PAPER

.

.   " How to Measure The Speed of a Very Large Object "

.

. This measurement is a " Speed of 24 Hours ". A speed of 24 hours is a distance in miles that a " Very Large Object " can travel in " One Hour " based on its " Size in Miles ". The braking point between " Speed and Distance " is the Point where an " Object " changes in " Size " from " Small to Large " . Small objects use a measurement of speed in " Miles Per Hour ", while " Large Objects " use a measurement of " Distance Traveled in Miles in an Hour " based on its size in Miles.

. Example : a small object would be a " Car " . Who's " Speed " is measured in " Miles per Hour ".

. Example : of a " Very Large Object " is the " Earth ". It is measured by " Distance Traveled " in " Miles In an Hour " based on its size in miles and distance covered in a " Period " of 24 hours.

. The Earth being 25,000 miles around at the " Equator ", will travel a distance of 25,000 miles in one " Rotation " in 24 hours at a " Speed of 24 hours " covering a distance of 1041.666667 miles in 1 hour based on its size of 25,000 miles around it.
. So to find out how " Big the Earth " is, take the distance of 1041.666667 miles x 24 hours and it will = 25,000 miles , the size of the " Earth " at the Equator.

. " Haley's Comet ", being 1,000,000 miles long traveling at a " Speed of 24 hours " moves a distance of 41,666.66667 miles in 1 hour based on it's size . It is a " Very Large Straight Object ", moving in a Circle with a " Diameter " of the Circle measuring 75 years or 2.7375 to the 10th power in miles.

. Equation : O = Dt 24

.

. O is the size of " A Very Large Object " in miles, determined by the " Distance of Travel" in 1 hour x 24 hours.

.

.   By: Will James

.

8

THE PAPER

.   Christ died on April 3, 33 A.D. at 6 a.m. . From January 1 to April 3 is 93 days. Now add them up = 31 days in Jan., 28 days in Feb., 31 days in March and 3 in to April total 9-3. This gives you the month and the day he was born on. 9 is the month which is September and 3 is the day of the month September 3th and the day of the week which was Tuesday.

From the " Forgotten Books of Eden ", in the " Secrets of Enoch " XXX " God " said, " And then I created all the Heavens, and the " Third Day was Tuesday " page 91. XXIX God said, " Then it became Evening and then again Morning and it was the Second Day ". " Monday is the First Day ".

Christ was born on September 3, 3 B.C. at 9:03 p.m. . His number is 3 3 3 . Christ was 36 years 8 months and 3 days old when he died, and as God said, " I am the " Alpha and the Omega" which is the " Beginning and the End ". Christ was born on the 3rd day Tuesday and died on the 3rd day Tuesday.

To get his number, take the 93 days from Jan. 1 to April 3 and divide 3 in to 9. It will go 3 times = 3,3,3. (note) " God " never gave a name to the " Second Day of the Week ", but when he created " Time "   there was 8 days in the " Week ". " The Second Day of The Week ", was " Time ", God set aside in every one's life to just in joy a little each " Day " of what " He Had Created ".

(note) When Jesus went into the wilderness the date was " September 5, 29 A. D. and at the end of the 40 days he spent there, the date was October 14, 29 A.D. He was 32 years old then. I would then be born 1945 years later on the same date October 14,1945.

Strange huh...

By: Will James

THE PAPER
" Strange Fate "

Death in Dallas

.

.   The First - of two " Strange Deaths " that put a city " Dallas, Texas " in the " Headlines " around the World , was the death of " President John F. Kennedy ", assassinated on Friday November 22, 1963, on a street in Dallas.

.

.   The Second - was the death of 7 " Astronauts ", when the " Space Shuttle, Columbia" blew up while returning to Earth over " Dallas, Texas " on Saturday Feb 1, 2003 at about
 8:00 a.m.   .
.   Both   " Days " were very much alike , one was Friday and the other was Saturday. Both had clear skies and warm days. They were 3 months apart, November to February, and both in a number 3 year 1963 and 2003, being 40 years apart. And me being a witness to both events.

.

.

B y: Will James.

THE PAPER

" Sun Light "
It's True Speed

.
.
.
.
.

The Sun burns 4 million tons of Hydrogen per second x 2,000 lbs. / ton = 8,000,000,000 lbs. / sec. x 86,400 seconds per day = 6.912 to the 14th power lbs. / day x 365 days / year = 2.52288 to the 17th power lbs. burned / year x 223,584,184.6 years old the age of the Earth as we know it, will = 5.640760676 to the 25th power lbs. of Hydrogen to light the Earth from Day 1 or 2.820380338 to the 22 power tons.177245.385 miles / second x 5,280 ft. / mile = 935,855,632.8 ft. / second Velocity. So it would take 8,000,000,000 lbs. / sec. of Hydrogen to generate a Velocity of 935,855,632.8 ft. / sec. = a burn of 8.548327028 lbs. / sec. burn / 1 ft. V / sec. which = 8.5 lbs. of Hydrogen / 1 ft. V / second. For light to reach the Earth, it took 8.7 min. which = 522 seconds burning Hydrogen at a rate of 8,000,000,000 lbs. / sec. which = 4.176 to the 12th power lbs. of Hydrogen to reach the Earth or 2,088,000,000 tons. A Mega Ton = is an explosive force equal to that of 1,000,000 tons of T N T. 1 foot = 0.3048 meters. 1 lb. of Astrolite G = 8600 meters / sec. V or 28,215.2231 ft. / sec. or 5.34792253 miles / sec. 1 lb. of T N T = 6900 meters / sec. V or 22,637.79528 ft. / sec. V or 4.287461226 miles / sec. V. (G) 1,000,000 lbs. x 28,215.2231 ft. / sec. V = 2.82152231 to the 10th power ft. / sec. V x 8,000,000,000 lbs. = 2.257217848 to the 20th power ft. / sec. V or 4.275033803 to the 16th power miles / sec. V (T N T) 1,000,000 lbs. x 22,637.79528 ft. / sec. V = 2.263779528 to the 10th power ft. / sec. V x 8,000,000,000 lbs. = 1.811023622 to the 22 power ft. / sec. V or 3.429968981 to the 16th power miles / sec. V. (H) 1,000,000 lbs. divided by 8.548327028 lbs. / ft. V / sec. = 116,981.9541 ft. / sec V x 8,000,000,000 lbs. = 9.358556328 to the 14th power ft. / sec. V divided by 5,280 ft. / mile = 1.77245385 to the 11th power miles / sec. V. " The True Speed of Sun Light ". In the Equation E=mc2, the Mechanical speed of light squared is 3.470769 to the 10th power.

The Mechanical speed of light = 186,300.000 miles / sec. The Mathematical speed of light squared is 3.14159264 to the 10th power or Pi to the 10th power. The Mathematical speed of light = 177245.385 miles / sec. The Speed of Sun Light squared is 3.14159265 to the 22 power or Pi to the 22 power. The Speed of Sun Light = 1.77245385 to the 11th power miles / sec. (Note) Page 11 of " The Paper " proves two things, First = is that 177,245.385 miles / sec. is the true Mathematical Speed of Light. Second = is that all sources of light do not travel at the same speed, but are regulated by the Energy Source powering it. (a) Mechanical Speed of Light = 186,300.000 miles / sec. (b) Mathematical Speed of Light = 177,245.385 miles / sec. (c) Speed of Sun Light = 1.77245385 to the 11th power miles / sec. E=mc2 ,the speed of Light Squared is (a) Mechanical speed = 3.4596 to the 10th power (b) Mathematical speed = 3.14159265 to the 10th power or Pi to the 10th power. (c) Sun Light speed = 3.14159265 to the 22 power or Pi to the 22 power.

(Note) The Speed of Sun Light 1.77245385 to the 11th power in miles x 31.536 days or 1 month = 5.589610461 to the 12th power in miles, one Light year.

On the other hand, 1 Sun Light year 5.589610961 to the 18th power in miles divided by 12 = 4.658008718 to the 17th power 1 Sunlight month. 1 Sunlight month 4.658008718 to the 17th power divide by 5.589610461 to the 12th power light year = 83,333.33333 or 83,333 years for light to travel as far as Sun Light can travel in 1 month.

If you divide 1 Sun Light year 5.589610961 to the 18th power in miles by 5.589610461 to the 12th power in miles in 1 light year it will = 1,000,000 years, the Time it would take Light to Travel as far as Sun Light can travel in 1 Sun Light Year.

[Note]

The other number they teach in school for the " Mathematical Speed of Light " is 299792.5 km/s. 299792.5 km/s x 0.621 = 186,171.1425 miles per second, the so called Mathematical Speed of Light which is just a number that really doesn't go anywhere. 300,000 km/s x 0.621 = 186,300.000 m/s, the Mechanical measurement of the Speed of Light.

By: Will James

THE PAPER
" The Age of The Universe "

.   The Age of the Universe is based on the " Diameter " of the " Sun ". The Diameter of the Sun is 863,190 miles around.

.   Take one Sun Light year 6.707532553 to the 13th power in miles x 863,190 the Diameter of the Sun in miles = 5.789875024 to the 19th power years old " The True Age of The Universe ".

[note]

I find it very strange that this is close to the same number of years estimated by " Science".

.

.

By: Will James

12

THE PAPER

" Time Travel "

The Age of the Earth by Sun Light.

.

.   Science has placed the Age of the Earth at or about 150,000,000 years old. The " Bible " has placed it at or about 7,000 years old. The Bible's 7,000 years old is 5,000 years B.C., and 2,000 years A.D. for a total of 7,000 years old.

.   Page 3 of " The Paper " showed that both are right and that Mr. Einstein's theory of " Time Travel " is more " Reality than Theory."

.   Through the use of the Mathematical Measurement of the " Speed of Sun Light ", I will show another way how the Earth Aged both by " Science " and " The Bible " because of the Reality of Sun Light powering " Time Travel ".

.   One Sun Light year by Mathematics is 5.589610461 to the 18th power in miles x 7,000 years = 3.912727323 to the 22 power in miles. The Earth being 25,000 miles around at the Equator, will travel 25,000 miles in 1 Revolution which takes 24 hrs.

24 hours equal's 1 day. So 25,000 miles x 365 days will equal 9,125,000 miles traveled in one year x 7,000 years will = 6.3875 to the 10th power in miles traveled in the " Bible's " 7,000 years in rotation.

.   Now take the 3.912727323 to the 22 power in miles in the " Bible's " 7,000 years and divide it by 6.3875 to the 10th power in miles of rotation in 7,000 years and it will = 6.125600505 to the 11 power in miles x 365 days in a year and it will equal 2.235844184 to the 14th power years old.

" The True Age of the Earth " by Sunlight. (note) 5.789875024 to the 19th power in years is the age of the Universe from page 12. Also noted by " Science ".

.

By: Will James

THE PAPER
" Strange Math "

The numbers on a " Roulette Wheel " are 1 to 36 . If added together they total 6 6 6 .

The number of the " Devil ".

" Pi " is 3.14159265 to the 10th power added together is 3 ,1,4,1,5,9,2,6,5 = 36 x 10 = 360 the degrees in a circle.

5.589610461 to the 18th power in miles in a Sun Light year divide by 25,000 miles the distance around the Earth = 2.235844185 to the 14th power years old, " The Age of the Earth " from page 13 of the Paper .

By: Will James

14

THE PAPER
" Is it Fact or Strange Coincidence "

Nostradamus named the " Third Antichrist ". His name is " Mabus ". If you change the A to an R and add an H, you have " Mr. Bush ". . In Rev. XIII: 18, the number of the " Beast " is the number of a man. This number is not in his name or his Social Security number as some would have you to believe. It's in his " Birthdate ". From the book " Nostradamus, Unpublished Prophecies ", Copyright © 1983 page 49, his quatrain says : The " Great Seer " doesn't tell us where or when the " Third Antichrist " will be born, but there are other clues : From the three water signs in " Astrology " will be born a man who will celebrate " Thursday ", as his Holiday. (note) this Thursday is always the third Thursday in November " Thanksgiving Day " a holiday of the " United States ". His renown praise, rule and power will grow on land and sea, bringing trouble to the " East ".

The Water Signs are " Scorpio, Cancer and Pisces " .

Mr. Bush was born under the sign of " Cancer " on 7 - 6 – 1946 – at 7 : 26. He was born with the number of the Devil 666 in his birthdate. If you add up the numbers in his birthdate = 7,6,19,46,7 and 26 they will total 111 . 111 x 6 = 666 . Again look at the date of his first year as President, it is 1-1-01 . He was born to be President at this " Time and Place ", in History.

Even the funds he was given, to run for President was $ 60,660,000. This quatrain goes on to say = Nostradamus indicates in French that the man will not be a Christian. That in itself does not mean that he will be the " Antichrist ", but the " Power " he will have does tell us that he will be strong enough to bring trouble (War) to the Orient or otherwise known as " The Middle East ".

[note]

President Bush was mostly referred to as Mr. Bush doing his Presidency.

By: Will James

15

THE PAPER

" A Strange Twist of Fate and The Philadelphia Experiment "

In 1922, a man named John David Thompson, was born in a small farm house in an Iowa corn field. In 1940, he joined the military and was put in the Army-Air Corps and was trained to be a fighter pilot. After training, he was stationed in Hawaii to undergo more training on an Aircraft Carrier in the Spring of 1941. On Dec.7, 1941, Japan declared War on the United States by bombing " Pearl Harbor ". Mr. Thompson was one of the very few Pilots who managed to get a fighter plane off the ground on that day and shot down enemy aircraft. Mr. Thompson received many commendations for his bravery on that day and was later transferred back state side to the " Philadelphia Naval Shipyard". He was chosen for a Top Secret Project called " Project Rainbow " and later to be known as " The Philadelphia Experiment ", which unbeknownst to the Navy, was a lesson in " Time Travel". Mr. Thompson was on board the Destroyer U.S.S. Eldridge on August 12, 1943 and through a Twist of Fate and an Experiment gone badly wrong, was sent back in Time and again was reborn in 1934 and was named Guy Thomas Strong and after graduating from College again joined the Navy and became a pilot. After retiring from the Navy, he became a Stunt Pilot and was flying in the making of the movie " Tora, Tora, Tora ", being filmed in Hawaii and based on the event of Dec.7th. And once again " Fate " would take a strange twist on Jan.13 1969. Mr. Guy Thomas Strong crashed and burned in a cane field, fighting the same War and losing his life this time around, trying to make a movie about the War he helped to Win in another life and another time, in the same place, " Pearl Harbor ".

[note]

As Mr. King would say: " Sometimes the Dead Will come back to claim their own ".

By: Will James

THE PAPER
" Evolution or Was it Just the Beginning of Time "

.

.   A Thousand years of Evolution will = 1 second of Earth Time. Evolution is just another one of " Nature's Mysteries " in " Time Travel ".

In the Beginning, when God created the " Heavens and the Earth, " He created two " Men ", not just one. The First = of these two men, was of an " Animal " like Nature, not knowing God or the ways of God. The Second = man was created by God's own hand and was already in the likeness of God and unlike " Evolutionary Man , " would know God and the ways of God. This man would then be called " Spiritual Man ". So it was in Genesis 1: 27 - God so then Created Man in his own image, creating them in male and female. This is what Science called " The Evolution of Mankind ".   In the Bible in " Genesis " this event accrued on the 6th day of " Creation " and a day being 24 hours in Earth Time and 24 hours will = 86,400 seconds, then a 1,000 years of Evolution would = 1 second of Earth Time. 86,400 seconds in 1 Earth day x 1,000 years of Evolution will = 86,400,000 Earth years or 1 Biblical day of Creation. The Bible states that God created the " Heavens and the Earth " in 6 Days. Then a Biblical day being 86,400,000 Earth years x 6 days will = 518,400,000 years of Evolution or Earth Time to Create . Which again makes both Science and the Bible " Right " or " Evolution " really was one of " Nature's Mysteries in Time Travel ". After the 6th day of Creation and the 7th day of Rest in " Genesis " chapter 2, the Lord God then formed a man of the " Dust of the Ground " and man became a living soul or what is called " Spiritual Man or Adam ", from which all the Descendants in the Bible would have come from. Here I find it very
" Strange ", that the Bible never again mentions "Evolutionary Man ".

.   But I find that the " Creation of Evolutionary Man ", would provide an answer to the ago old question that the Bible does not tell you " The Answer Too ",   If Adam and Eve really were the only two people on the Earth in the Beginning and they only had two sons at first, then who would they have Married, to help start the " Population of the Earth ? ".

By: Will James

THE PAPER
" Two Worlds of Reality "

.   The best way I can explain why I live in two Worlds or Time periods at the same Time, is to find the connecting link. I now know that I, too, was somehow a part of the Philadelphia Experiment and was one of the persons who never came back on the day of the   experiment.

.   It was said and claimed to have happened on Aug.12, 1943. Some say it was October and most likely it was October 28, 1943 time 10:00 a.m. Wednesday. The movie that was made about it went with October too. I now believe that October 28, 1943 to be the true date as I did not return on that day, but was reborn in the Future 2 years later on November 8,1945. That would make connection # 1.

.   In 1951, my family moved to Denver, Colorado and as I did not turn 6 years old till November of that year, I had to wait till the start of the next school year which then was Sept. 1952. So in April 1953, I am now 7 ½ years old and in the " First Grade ".

The date is April 15, 1953, time is 12:00 noon and I am at home sick and laying on my bed looking out the window at a light pole across the alley from my home and I am asking myself what if I could see into the Future. This is the early 50's and Time Travel and the Future were words that a 7 ½ year old kid had never heard of. I was just learning to read in the first grade and all I knew about then was a little boy and girl named Dick and Jane and a dog and cat named Spot and Puff. Connection # 2 comes here, as Denver and the Philadelphia shipyard are on the exact same parallel line, the 40 degree parallel and the effects from that experiment on October 1943 are still circling the Earth 10 years later on April 15,1953 following a path along the 40th parallel and once again the Navy on this date toke a new ship called the USS Timmerman as part of an experiment to test the effects of a small, high-frequency generator providing 1,000 hz instead of the larger standard 400 hz lower frequency type generator as first used in the USS Eldridge, causing its effects to drew me once again back in to the Future and in to the World I now know.

Now in connection # 3, after the " Philadelphia Experiment " went badly wrong, the equipment used in the experiment was secretly moved to a small air base at Montauk, New York and then renamed " The Montauk Project ".

In a book called The Montauk Project " Experiments in Time " chapter 12 page 89 and 90 it said, Essentially, what the scientists were doing was using the 1943, 1963 1983 vortex, which was based upon the natural twenty year biorhythms of the Earth. 1943, 1963 and 1983 acted as anchor points for the main vortex.

.   Sub vortices or open ended vortices would be created by going from the main one through an anchor point (43, 63 or 83). The Montauk anchor point, August 12, 1983 was used.

.   For example, let's say they wanted to reach Nov. 1981. There would be a bridge point from November of 1981 to August 12, 1983. From August 12, 1983 they could go to whatever Time they wanted . The vortex ran between August 12, 1943 and August 12, 1983.

.   In chapter 13 " Time Travel ", the project changed hands so to speak. On page 91 it says, as most of the technicians were gone, a new technical crew was brought in. I don't know who they were and what their qualifications were, but they were called the " Secret Crew ", the project was restarted and is now sometimes referred to as " Phoenix III." This lasted from February 1981 until 1983.

.   The objective now was to explore " Time " itself. The crew began to look at " Past history and to the Future ", just scouting around. Those who traveled through the vortex described it as a peculiar spiral tunnel that was lit, all the way down. As one started to walk down, he would suddenly be pulled through it. It propelled one out the other end, usually in another place (as opposed to Montauk) or according to where the transmitter was set or placed. It could be anywhere in the Universe.

.   The tunnel resembled a corkscrew with an effect similar to light bulbs. It was a fluted sort of structure and not a straight tunnel. It twisted and took turns until you'd come out the other end. There, you would meet somebody or do something. You would complete your mission and return. The tunnel would open for you, and you'd come back to where you came from. However, if they lost power during the operation, you would be lost in Time or abandoned somewhere in the vortex itself.

.   Now you will know and understand the " Secret of The Grassy Knoll ". On the night of   Nov 21,1963, I was standing at a Race Track in Dallas, Texas called the " Devil's Bowl " and there was a terrible accident on the track and I had to look away from it and happen to look over the sky line of downtown Dallas. It was so Black, it was not like anything you have ever seen, it was like looking into a " Black Hole in Space ". Till now I never understood just what it was I saw that night. It was a Vortex in Time and they sent someone through " Time " that could not be traced, to kill President Kennedy the next day, Nov. 22,1963 as it would also be in a 20th biorhythm year 1963. It was always stated that there was a second shooter in a tree on the " Grassy Knoll " his shot was hard, but he was never seen and never found. As you read in the above paragraph you could go through the vortex tunnel, meet someone or complete a mission and then return. Someone in the government wanted him dead and took a trip in to the " Future " and seen that Lee Harvey Oswald's shot would only wound him and so they sent in a second shooter to make sure that he was killed and then they could lose him in Time and keep the " Secret of the Grassy Knoll, " " a secret forever, till Now ".

Based on true Facts

By: Will James

THE PAPER

" A Strange Gift or Was It Really Looking Into The Future ? "

On page 18, I stated that on the night of Nov. 21, 1963, I was at a Race Track in Dallas, Texas when a very bad accident occurred. Having to look away from it, I was a witness to a " Vortex's In Time ". What I did not know at the time was, somehow I knew that someone was going to die very soon. That person was President John F. Kennedy, shot to death the next day on Nov. 22, 1963, about 10 blocks from where I was working at the time.

It was not until 19 years later that I really learned that somehow I could do something very strange that I was told all my life couldn't be done. I learned that I could write or know when someone was going to die or in another very strange twist of " Fate " those that were to die, I could write and they would live just as I had written.

The First of 11 people to die and then there were 32, then 9 more, was a lady who lived on the other side of the World, by the name of Princess Grace or Mrs. Grace Kelly movie " Star ". She had a very bad car accident and was in the hospital with the very best of care that anyone could get. I for some unknown reason wrote " that within the week, She would Die ", and within that week, she died just as I had written. She died on Sept. 13, 1982.

The Second person to die was my sister's father in law. His name was Mr. Johnson. Mr. Johnson had gotten sick and was taken to the Hospital. My sister never said what was wrong with Mr. Johnson, but again for no reason, I wrote, " He will die within the next week ", and on the Sunday of that week, he died just as I had written. He died on Sept. 19, 1982.

The Third person to die was my sister's father. After writing about the Death of Mr. Johnson, I again for no reason wrote, " My sister's father will also Die, within the same week as Mr. John-son ", and just as I wrote, he killed himself on Friday of the same week at 9:00 a.m. I was on my way back from Houston, Texas about 11:00 a.m. that morning, when an old pickup truck passed me and I heard a loud pop like a gun shot that rang in my ear. I thought it was a backfire from the old pickup truck as it passed by. I never thought any more about it till I got back to the water plant with the load I was carrying for it. I was met by my boss and was told that my sister's father had killed himself that morning at 9:00 a.m. with a gun and the pop I heard at 11:00 a.m. was not a back fire from the old pickup truck, but a gunshot 200 miles away when her father shot himself in the head. He died Sept 24, 1982.

The Fourth person to die was a friend of mine and my boss at work. Mr. Williams had been sick with cancer of the Blood. I had been working with Mr. Williams for about 5 years when he died. Mr. Williams had taken sick a year or so after going to work with me and was taking 2 pints of blood every Monday and every one though he was doing ok. In June of 1988, for no reason I wrote, " In The Month of April, In The Middle Of The Month, Mr. Williams Will Die ". In the very next year in the month of April, in the middle of the month, Mr. Williams went into the hospital on a Monday just like every Monday, to get his blood and at 2:00 p.m. on that day he got very sick and died . The Doctors never knew what happened to Mr. Williams on that day causing him to die, but died just as I had written the year before. He died on April 24, 1989.

The Fifth person to die was my brother. This is the " Strangest Death " yet. In January 1996, I took my check book out one day and started to mark the days of the month that I would get paid on. I had marked the months all the way down to June 14, 1996. I stopped there, as that would take me half way through the year. I never knew that when I was marking the days and stopped on June 14,1996 that, that would be the last day of a 23 year career working for a City and the week that my brother would die. He died on June 11, 1996 at 11:00 a.m., I lost my job in that same week on June 14, 1996.

The Sixth person in this true story was wrote in to History by me. His real " Fate " is still unknown to the World. This person's name is Osama Bin Laden . Mr. Bin Laden was an Al Qaeda Terrorist who on Sept 11,2001 attacked the United States by hijacking Airplanes and flying them into the World Trade Center Buildings in New York City. In November of that year I wrote on a message board on the Internet " On April 29,2002, " Mr. Bin Laden Will Pass In To History By His Own Hand ", I signed it " The Left Hand Of The Devil." I received an email back in a few days after posting it from someone. They had sent an email written somehow so it could not be printed out of the email. It was so frightening that I cannot remember all that was said, but I do remember this few words " We Shall See ". In the month of March 2002, the United States Army said they were getting close to getting Mr. Bin Laden, but again just like I wrote after April 29, 2002, Mr. Bin Laden has not been seen or heard from in real life anywhere in this World. There are some Governments that would like you to believe that he is alive and well, but no one has shown any real living proof that he is. He passed in to History on April 29, 2002, just like I wrote he would.

The Seventh person to die was a man by the name of Mr. Heckerman, of N.C. Mr. Heckerman was unknown to me, but was a friend of a lady I knew on the internet. She told me, she met and fell in love with him in another life and had found him again in this life. One night we were talking on line and she was upset because he would not talk to her, so not really believing that I really could write that people would die as I had written, I wrote that, " With In The Week He Would   Die ". I never told the lady what I had done, till 3 weeks later she found me on line and told me that a friend of hers had called that day and told her that Mr. Heckerman had died of a Heart Attack 3 weeks earlier. I then had to tell her what I did the night we were talking and that she was so upset that I wrote that Mr. Heckerman would die within the week and he did just as I had written. He died in 2004.

The Eighth person to die was no one I knew. I had another friend who was married to a man who drank a lot. So one night while I was talking to her on the net, I wrote, " That he would Die, within the month ". It was with that, I learned whatever it was I was doing, it was not to be played around with. The man that I wrote that was to die that time never died, but another man working in a deep ditch in a City close to a city where I work, died that month and had been working in a deep ditch being dug up by a friend of mine that I had worked with on another job a few years be for. He died in 2004.

The Ninth person to die was my sister, the daughter in law of Mr. Johnson. Three weeks before I told my boss that I was giving him 3 weeks' notice that a Safety Inspection Sticker on our other Dump Truck would run out at the end of the month , and again like my brother , I didn't know that I was again counting the days, till the end of my sister's life. Another strange thing about this death was that when she got home I was going to ask her for a credit card back that I had given to her in her name, it was " The American Express Card " and was going to close it out as I was tired of worrying about if she had the money at the end of the month to pay the bill on it, it came to its end along with her life and the truck's sticker ran out just like I know it would She died on July 27, 2005, at 9:30 a.m. Another Strange thing about this death is that about 20 years ago her brother, that was the Fifth person to die in this story, was with me in Dallas, Texas one Saturday at an open house given by J.B. Hunt Transportation Company. He and I was looking at a new truck right out of the box as they say, when a man from Hunt trucking walked up and said, " You boys thank you can drive this truck" I then said jokingly, " No Sir ", why not said the man , I said, " This is a new truck, we have never driven a new one, we would set up there and go to sleep and run off the road and kill ourselves .We are used to seeing the Highway through the Floorboard and the Sky through the roof and having to stop every 50 miles and work on the trucks.

So with that, strangely enough the truck that my Sister was driving for J. B. Hunt was a new one right out of the box and had only been on the road about 3 1/2 months, but she did not die like we may have, she had to drive her truck off the highway to avoid hitting a car in front of her that had a tire blow out. It would end up costing her own life just like I knew it would, when she first set foot in that new truck driving for J.B. HUNT Transport.

[note]

A very strange fact about the American Express Card I gave to my sister in her name, was that I did not know till a year after her death, that on the back where you sign your name, is a number of which a part of this number, is part of the account number from the front of the card and some other numbers for who knows what. The other numbers, I am talking about, were 1 0 1 4   888. In the game of poker, the ACE card can count as 1 or 11. In the Old West Wild Bill Hickok was killed while playing poker and when someone took a look at the cards he was holding, his hand was
" Ace's and 8's ". He was holding two pair of Ace's and 8's and it was also said that all of these cards were black and the fifth card was not know for certain what or color it was.

Later they named his hand " The Dead Man's Hand " . Strangely enough the two 1's in the last part of her number on back of this card, represents " The two Ace's with three 888's ", The Dead Man's Hand.................All of these numbers, were also printed in " Black Ink "............ Strange huh or was it maybe, just " Luck of The Draw ".

The Tenth person to die, was my daughter-in-law, Susan. She had just had a birthday and on Saturday Feb. 17, 2007, my wife and I had taken her and my wife's son, out to lunch at a Steak House, in Rock Wall, Texas. Susan was feeling pretty good that day, but due to health problems had to use a wheelchair to get around. When we all went out to lunch together, I would be the one to roll her in and out of the restaurants. After lunch while rolling Susan back to the car, I again for some unknown reason wrote, " That within a week, she would die ", and on Wednesday Feb 21, while trying to get from her bed to her wheel chair she fail and hit her head on the wall beside her bed. An ambulance was called for and the ambulance attendant asked her if she would like to be taken to the hospital and she replied no, she just had a headache and would be ok. On Friday 2 days later, my wife's son came home from work and found Susan lying part way off her bed and would not respond to him and was rush to the hospital and then had to go on by care flight, to Tyler, Texas, where on Saturday morning Feb 24, 2007, she died at 9:00 a.m. just like I wrote she would, the Saturday before.

The Death of 32

I returned to that same Steak House with my wife and her son a month later, after Susan's death. We happen to park in the same parking spot as we did on that Saturday Feb 17, 2007 the day that Susan was with us and as we were walking back to the car after lunch, I happen to walk down the same path that I had rolled Susan down and a very " Ghost Filling " came over me like it was " Death It Self ". I could somehow feel a very strong and strange energy that started in my left hand and traveled up my arm. The first thing I said to myself was, " I wonder who is going to die
now ". The date was March 17, 2007 and again this 17th fell on a Saturday. The feeling I got on that day being unknown to me , was from an energy source being generated by " 32 Students " who would all be " Dying together in the Future " a month later, 1200 miles away, on Monday April 16, 2007, just one day away from the 17th of the month again, and one day after Saturday, when a male student named Seung-Hui Cho, would chain 3 Exit doors closed to the class rooms and begin shooting and killing these students, at the University of Virginia Tech. (6 - 16 - 16)

[note]

*Up Date to this True Story

On the first anniversary of this shooting, April 15, 2008, I learn that the strange energy I was feeling in my left hand on March 17, 2007, was the Gunshot to the left hand of a girl name Kaylyn in the class room of Virginia Tech, who would be shot a month later, on April 16, 2007. Another strange thing on this same note, is the day before the first anniversary of this shooting, on April 15, 2008, I learned the first name of a friend of mine, I had known for a long time, her name was Kaylyn, the same first name as the girl that was shot. I have to ask how much Stranger is this going to get...........

The Death of 9 More

It was June 16, 2007, my wife asked if we could go back once again to the Steak House, in Rock Wall, Texas for lunch. June 16 was on Saturday, one day from the 17th on Sunday. Again I parked in the same parking spot as before, as I wanted to see if I could feel the energy, I had before on March 17, 2007. After lunch while returning to the car, I again walked down the same path I had before, but did not feel anything. I told myself, I guess no one is going to die this time. Then on June 19, 2007, 3 days later there were 9 Firefighters killed in Charleston, South Carolina fighting a large store fire, which this time was 1017 miles from where I live. Here again just returning to that location on the date 6 – 16, in itself foretold the death of 9 more people that would be dying all together. (6 – 16 – 16)

The Eleventh person to die was a friend of mine, named Bill , who I had worked with for 23 years. His death is a " Strange " one too. On Sunday July 1, 2007, I was going through some old papers in my desk and I found an email that was sent to me a long time ago about the deaths of the Presidents elected in a year ending with a " 0 ". I was thinking that this would make a good addition to my paper with a little reworking. The last president on this list, last name starts with the letter " B ". He is still alive today. On Tuesday July 3, after getting home from work, I had set down to read the local newspaper of which I hardly ever read and happen to see the " Obituaries " where there was a picture of my friend, whose first name started with the letter " B ", had died on Sunday July 1, 2007, the same day I had wrote about the presidents dying. Another strange thing about this is that Bill had the same middle initial " R " as I do and the first letter in his last name as I do " W " and was born on a Saturday in the same year as I was, 1945 on January 13 and died on the same day of the week, that I was born on, " Sunday ", on October 14, 1945, which would make him 10 months and 1 day older than me. " Cause of Death Unknown ". This happened just 1 day after I was at a " Psychic " meeting on a Saturday June 30, 2007, trying to learn how I could do this and had shown this page to 2 friends at the meeting. Is this some kind of a clue that maybe my own number could be coming up soon too, just wondering..........

Then The Death of 5 more

On Feb 13, 2008, I was thinking the next day was Susan's birthday, as my wife's son had asked if we would like to go back to the Steak House in Rock Wall, Texas on Saturday Feb.16 for lunch to celebrate her birthday. The next day would be Thursday Feb 14 , " St Valentine's Day ". I said to myself, I wonder if anyone else would be dying on or close to her birthday, as it was a year ago, on a Saturday Feb 17, that I wrote, that she would be dying within the next week, as her birthday was on Feb.16 and not the 14th, as I was thanking. On Feb 14, 2008, there was another massacre of 8 more students, killing 5 of them at a university called, " Northern Illinois University " in Dekalb, Ill., 2 days before her birthday, on Saturday Feb 16th. The young man doing the killing, had been a student there and was said to have bought his guns online from the same Gun Dealer, as the young man in the Virginia Tech killings, which was not far from where this killing had taken place, 1 year later. This young man's name was, " Steven Kazmierczak ." Here again the number 16 and the day, Saturday played a very " Strange " part in these people dying and again somehow I knew, but again, really would not believe that it really was going to happen. (6 - 16 - 16)

[note]

The above story happened very much like the real story of a gangster, named Al Capone, who on Feb 14, 1929, St. Valentine's Day, massacred 7 men, in North Chicago, Illinois. As " Strange Luck " would have it, the name of the this school was, " Northern Illinois University ", also in Illinois and like 1 year, happening in a year, ending with a " 9 ", like the first massacre in Chicago in 1929, but counting the number of years between the 2 dates, 1929 and 2008, it did end in a " 9 ", " 79 " years later. Strange huh........We also did not go to the Steak House this time, due to a bad storm, on Saturday, Feb 16, 2008.

(up date 5 - 2 - 2011)   In page 19, the Sixth person in this true story, in the end, did pass into History, just like I wrote he would. This person was Osama Bin Laden, an Al Qaeda Terrorist who had attack the United States on Sept 11, 2001. In November of 2001, I wrote on a message board on the Internet " On April 29,2002, Mr. Bin Laden Will Pass In To History By His Own Hand ". It ended up taking 10 years before this prediction came to pass, as the military had just missed capturing Mr. Bin Laden just before April 29, of 2002 and he went into hiding for the next 10 years, and then was finally located as strange luck would have it, again on April 29, 2011. An order was given to a highly trained team of Navy Seals, to capture or kill Mr. Bin Laden, but they had to delay this mission by one day till the date of April 30, 2011, due to bad weather and then upon coming face to face with him, was told to surrender. Mr. Bin Laden then refused, leaving the Navy Seals no choice but to kill him by firing two shots to his head, and then was rushed to an Aircraft Carrier and buried at sea on MAY 1, 2011, passing into History by his own hand, by not giving up. Another strange thing about the date April 29th, when Mr. Bin Laden set the date of Sept 11, to cause the death of some 3,000 Americans, he was also marking the last part of the date of his own death with the number 11. That date would then read, April 29, 11.

The Death of a Dictator

On the night of October 19th, 2011, I took a deck of poker cards and after reshuffling them two times, I then cut the deck in half and pulled 3 cards off the top. I then laid them face down in a roll and then, I turned them up one at a time, the cards were 10 of Diamonds, the Ace of Spades and the Queen of Spades. The Ace of Spades in Fortune Telling, foretells " Death ". As I had laid the three cards down on a desk calendar, I was going to write down which 3 cards they were on the date for that day, October 19th, as I had laid down once again, the Card of Death, but in doing so, I mistakenly wrote them down on the date of October 20th, what I had done unknowingly to me was, I had just foretold the date of the Death of one of the most hated men in the World, The Dictator of Libya, Moammar Gaddafi, who was killed on this date October 20, 2011 by his own people who he had terrorized for 42 years. The card, The Queen of Spades, had also foretold the Death of one of his female BodyGuards, who was killed trying to protect him.

Everything I have written here is a " True Fact " and is a " True Story " and a Story that had to be told. It is just one of the Strange things that happen to me in my life. I look every day for the reason " Why " .

By: Will James

THE PAPER

" Changing The Future or Was It Really Witchcraft ? "

On page 19, something very strange happened to me. Looking back in to my life, I learned that somehow, I had the ability to write when someone was going to die. Again it is another clue into my very strange life of " Time Travel and the Two Real Worlds of Reality " that I live in.

It is hard to understand how anyone could have the ability to do something like that . If you were to go back in Time about a few hundred years, they would call that kind of ability " Witchcraft " and you would be burned alive. Down through History , there were a lot of people killed for what some believed was " Witchcraft " and for what really was just someone's way of trying to get even with someone or a lot of people . In my research of " Witchcraft " I found the only real and true person , who I believe to be a real and true " Witch " was Mother Shipton, she was born Ursula Sontheil in 1488 in a cave beside the river Nidd in North Yorkshire, England. Close by was an ancient well with supposed mystical powers.

The woman who came to tend to her 15 year old mother, Agatha, spoke of a smell of sulfur and a great crack of thunder as the child came into the world. The baby was born misshapen and huge. Some thought her father was the " Devil ". Her mother gave her up at the age of two and supposedly went to live in a convent for the rest of her life.

Her hometown was in Knaresborough ,England. Her power to see into the Future made her well known not only in her hometown , but throughout England. Many of her visions came true within her own lifetime and in subsequent centuries. Mother Shipton predicted important historical events many years ahead of their time – the Great Fire of London in 1666, the defeat of the Spanish Armada in 1588 – as well as the advent of modern technology. She even predicted her own death in 1561. Today her prophecies are still proving uncannily accurate. She wrote her prophecies like poems. She died in 1561.

I truly, at times, didn't believe that the ability that I had was real. On page 19, proof came that night, when my friend told me that the man she loved in another life and had again found in this life wouldn't talk to her. She told me that a friend of hers, had told her that day, that he had died 3 weeks before. Not believing this ability was real, I had written that he would die within the week, and after she told me he had died 3 weeks earlier from a heart attack. I knew then, it could only be real.

" Fate " would again take another strange twist. Believing that " Death " was all I could write about, I soon learned that I could write " Life " too.

That came one day, when I was reading a paper I get once a week. It is called " Weekly World News ".The date on this paper is October 1,2002. A columnist and America's Sexiest Psychic writer for the News, was told by a fellow psychic, and this is from her printed column on page 27, said Dear Serena : I am a fellow psychic who is writing to warn you that I have seen a dark and disturbing aura around your column for the last four months. It gets darker as the weeks go by, and I am fearful that it means tragedy for your loved ones – such as your sister Sonya – and, of course, your faithful readers.

You share so much with the world with your selfless advice and wise psychic guidance that I urge you to look into your crystal ball for some warning concerning your own life, Serena…. This message is sent with love and care and in the hopes that you will listen and be very cautious. I fear your time with us on Earth may be running out quickly. Sign – Worried For You in Sedona.

Dear Worried: My sincere thanks for your concern, but I honestly don't believe it's needed. I receive several letters similar to yours every year, but I haven't yet seen the warnings come true. I place my faith and God – given psychic ability in helping others and trust that the Universe will take care of me.

As soon as I finished reading that, I wrote, " Serena will live a long and happy life. " In the next week's paper dated October 8, 2002, page 8 it says " Serena ignored a premonition of great danger just last week in the paper dated October 1,2002. On page 8 the headlines read, " PSYCHIC SERENA SABAK INJURED IN CAR WRECK " ……… and in critical condition, say docs.

This is the story by George Sanford, Weekly World News. --- Boca Raton, Fla. – Weekly World News psychic and columnist Serena Sabak 36, is in critical condition after a drunk driver plowed into her car.

Co-workers were shocked to learn of the accident and offered their wishes for a speedy recovery for the famous newspaper psychic. " Serena is a very special person," says WWN Associate Art Director Tim Kelly, a longtime friend. " She's an important part of WWN, and we hope she returns to us soon."

Authorities say that the collision occurred when a drunk driver lost control of his vehicle and sideswiped Serena's car as she drove south on I-95 just after 11 p.m. on " September 25. " She was rushed to an undisclosed hospital. " She's fighting for her life," one doctor says. But her will to live is very strong."

The other motorist, whose name is being with-held, suffered superficial injuries and could face charges of reckless driving, authorities say. Ironically, the psychic did not heed forewarnings of her own Fate. She told me that several readers had written to tell her they'd had premonitions about impending danger and she herself had a recurring dream about being in a car wreck in the weeks before it happened, reveals her tearful kid sister, Sonya Sabak,31, who shares an apartment with Serena. That night I told her that I was having a bad feeling about her leaving the apartment. But Serena had promised a reader who thought his cat was possessed that she was going to say a healing prayer at his home and she always lived up to her word.

The Doctors later said they could not understand how anyone could live through an accident like that one. Serena, was in coma for many weeks and it looked like all hope was about gone for her, so I wrote her a letter and said this from a " Witchcraft " book I had once and this is the only thing I ever got to read from it, as after I read it, the book vanished a few days later and was never seen again. It said, " So Radiant Was Her Beauty , That Death Itself Would Lay Down It's Sword and Shield At Her Feet ". I then told Serena , " To pick up that Sword and fright her way back into the light and defeat the Evil that is trying to take her life." I signed the letter, " I Am Nobody really . "

In the December 10, 2002 paper, her sister Sonya said, " We Did It, ". As you no doubt know by now, my big sister, Serena , is out of her coma and on the road to recovery, thanks to the group prayer led by me and spoken by all the WWN readers. Once again, I've pulled Serena's fat out of the fire.

[note]

As you can see from the dates on the papers, I knew nothing about her accident before October 1, when I got my paper and wrote: " That Serena would live a long and happy life." As it was in the next week's paper of October 8, that it said she was in a car wreck on Sept 25 and that was13 days before the paper dated October 8 had come out with the story about it. So did I somehow cross " Time It Self ", or " Did I Change Her Future ", by writing, " That She Would Live A Long and Happy Life " or " Could It Have, Really Been Witchcraft ", and Like Mother Shipton , maybe my father was the " Devil " too……… based on all true Facts by Will James

Life Number Two

In the Spring of 2005, a friend of mine, named Ben, was again like Serena Sabak , was in a very bad car accident and was in a coma for two weeks. He and a friend were on their way to Tyler, Texas, when another car caused them to run off the highway and wreck out. He and his friend were rushed to the hospital. His wife and his family along with his friend's family waited at the hospital and was about to lose all hope for his recovery, till I again wrote " He Will Live A Long and Happy Life ". A few days later after writing that, I heard he had come out of the coma and was going to recover.

Based on true Facts by Will

James

[note]

*Update to this True Story

Date 1-14-06   I went to Tyler, Texas today to see my wife who had fallen down some steps at home the day before and had to be rushed that night to the hospital in Tyler by air. When the plane got there it was met by an ambulance and one of the ambulance attendants was the son of Ben in this true story, and he ask my wife where she was from and she told him she was from Terrell and he ask her if she knew his father and mother there and she said, yes she knew them very well and that his father had been in an accident in Tyler some time back and he said yes and that his father was well now and back home with his mother and they were very happy now and they had moved from Terrell to another town, that just so happen to be where my other sister has live now for a number of years. "Here again is proof that I changed someone's " Future ", by the power in what I wrote or Just What was it I Did ? . Maybe only the " Devil " Knows huh……

Life Number Three

On or about April, 07 the sister of my other daughter in law, who smoked a lot, got very sick and went into the Hospital. Her condition was getting worse and my daughter in law called my wife and said she was afraid that she was going to lose her sister and I too did not have much hope for her after hearing how sick she really was. Then she somehow got better for a few days, and things started to look a little better for her, then once again she took a very bad turn for the worst and was a lot more worse this time than before and even the doctors were thinking she would not make it back this time, so my daughter in law called my wife back again and said she was asking everyone to help " Pray " for her. So without saying anything to anyone about it, I took her sister's love for her and the " Strange Power " that I have, in the things that I write and I wrote: " She is to live a long life " and now she is getting better every day and is in rehab and a few weeks later she was able to go back home..... Again, a true story.

Life Number Four

I received an E-mail from Dr. Patricia, stating that one of the members in our group, Sister Mary's 10 year old Daughter, was under a Psychic attack and they have had to commit her to keep her from committing Suicide. Your Prayers, Blessings, Energy or whatever it is the Spirit put on your Heart to do to handle this matter is already Appreciated.

After reading this Email, I once again wrote this from the Witchcraft Book that I had once = " So Radiant Was Her Beauty, That Death Itself Would Lay Down Its Sword And Shield At Her Feet." I Then Told " The Little Girl " To Pick Up That Sword And Fight Her Way Back Into The Light And Defeat The Evil That Is Trying To Take Her Life. Then I wrote " She is to live a long and happy life. I will again sign this, " I am Nobody really ".......

A True Story

By: Will James

THE PAPER

God said, " Save But One Soul, and I Shall Save Yours "

This is what God once told me. Somehow I always knew that I was not like my other brothers and sisters. And with the death of my youngest sister I also learned that she too was not like the others. I once told her that she was much like me, as I always wondered what made the world go round.

I have always had to walk on the " Dark Side " of life and walk where " Angels " would fear to tread. I knew and met robbers and killers in my lifetime of which one was a man by the name of " Richard Speck ". I met Richard in a Café in East Dallas in the Spring of 1965. He had just got out of Huntsville Prison. His wife Shirley was working at the Café with my cousin. Richard was mean to his wife then and I guess he must have just hated women all together, as in the summer of 1966 while in Chicago waiting for a job on a Merchant Marine Ship, he went on a rampage killing 8 nursing students.

I was in Hawaii at the time, as my cousin had met a young man in Dallas and had married him and he ended up being stationed there in the Army. Being alone in Hawaii and wanting to make friends with people in Hawaii, I went to a Church one Sunday and the very next week a very bad Storm came up and destroyed that Church.

I guess that was a way for " Satan " to tell me that I was not to make friends with those people and I never went back to Church again. I returned to Texas 8 years later. I tried to always do right in everything I did, but things never seem to go right somehow.

I sent money to my cousin, to buy in to a company she and her husband had, and after a month they ended up losing a contract and I lost all my money I had sent them. I went to see them with the intent of killing her husband, and on the night I got to the city where they lived, God spoke to me that night and told me that the money I lost was not worth that man's life. You may think right here in this " True Story ", by not killing him, that I saved a soul. Well, we will never know as I never again ever saw or spoke to him.

I began to wonder years later, how someone like me could save a soul after walking with the " Devil " all my life. It all began one night a few years ago, when my youngest sister called me from Wyoming and told me, she and a friend of hers were helping her friend's brother take their father's body back home for burial and they had a wreck and her friend's brother was killed and she wanted to ask me if she could borrow $50 or $60 as she and her friend had spent all they had for gas on the trip. I said yes, and the next morning,

I wired her $300. Up till then, I had not seen or heard from my sister in a lot of years, and really did not know her all that well, as I had left home when she was only 3 years old, and was only in and out of her life very briefly. We became very close after that, always talking on the internet and I soon learned that I would end up taking care of her the last few years of her life.

She could not hold a job for very long at a time. She told me she didn't like to be told what to do all the time, so she went back to driving trucks coast to coast as there she was very much her own boss. After driving about a year for a company that I hoped was a good one, she was let go and told she was not doing her job.

I know better than that I told her, what the company wanted was for her to run over her log time and she would not do that as it was breaking the law. She was worried about losing that job as I had told her, if you can drive for 2 years without any tickets or accident you can drive for any one you like. After looking around for a few days and about to lose hope she went on the internet and found a company called J.B. Hunt Transport. That was about September of 2004.

She was living in Colorado Springs at the time. After driving for J.B. Hunt for a few months and things looked like they were going well for her, she got sick on the road and had to go into the Hospital. She recovered in about a month and was able to go back to work. The friend she was staying with was wanting her to move out, so she asked me to help her move back home to Texas. So I took a vacation and went to Colorado to help her. That was April 15,2005 and was the beginning of the " Last Days " of her life.

After spending the weekend in Colorado, we left on Monday and got back early on Tuesday morning. We spent the rest of that day getting her set up here and the next day, she called her new boss at J.B. Hunt Transport and ask if she could have one of the new trucks they had gotten in. They told her they would see, and in a few days, they called her back and told her to pick up her new truck.

I carried her to their yard in Dallas, and after driving around their yard looking for it, we finally found it. It was the prettiest truck in the yard, and was brand new right out of the box, as they say. She was like a kid with a new toy. The first thing she did was to start the engine.

I helped her load all her personal things in the cab of the truck and told her when she got a load going somewhere, come back to Terrell and I would give her a new C.B. Radio. She was then on her way back on the road, and would be out for 14 days at a time and back home for 4 days. Things were going well for her, but we were having problems keeping up with each other by email, so I got her a cell phone and told her to call me every day, just to say that, " I love you " . That was the first of June. She could not wait to get home to get her phone. She would keep asking me: what does it look like? I just told her: you will love it, it retails for $ 450.00, but again we were having problems talking to each other, and when she got back home the second time out, I asked her about it and she said, I tried, but we were out of range.

It was Sunday July 17th, and would be the last time I would ever get to talk to my sister, she called me and we talked for about an hour about this and that and about what we was going to do someday, and then she told me, she had put in to stay out on the road this time for the whole month, as I said before, she was to stay out for only 14 days. I told her that was a long time to stay out without rest, and she said, " Do you want Me To Come In? ", and it was at that moment in " Time " that I held her " Life " and " Soul " in my hands, I said " yes, but you need the money in your checking account, you are broke," She then said, she would go ahead and stay out then", …….. and now I will have to live with what I said to her, " For the rest of my life."

What happened next was, by saying what I said to her, changed her " Future " and the remaining " Time ", that she had left in her life. It put into motion an event in the " Future ", that would take place just south of a town, called Seymour, Indiana on July 27,2005 at 9:30 a.m. and would become one of the worst " Truck Wrecks " in the State of Indiana's history, when a car with 3 women and a child in it , would have a blow out in front of her truck. She would then have to drive her truck off the highway to keep from killing the women and the child in the car and by doing so, saved their lives, but losing her own life. As God said " The Greatest Thing A Human Being Can Do, Is Give His or Her Life To Save Another Human Being's Life."

Now another " Strange Twist " in this already strange story, three weeks later, after her death, I received 4 boxes from J.B. Hunt Transport, containing what was left of her personal things. The first day, I just looked through the boxes, not paying much attention to what was in them. One evening, I took a second look at them, and came across a book called " THE PURPOSE DRIVEN LIFE " What On Earth Am I Here For ? by Rick Warren.

In the first part of the book called, " What On Earth Am I Here For ?, under day 3 " What Drives Your Life ", page 27, I read down to page 35 and at the end of the 3rd day, it says " Day Three Thinking About My Purpose." ……… Point to Ponder: Living on purpose is the path to peace…….. Verse to Remember : " you, Lord, give perfect peace to those who keep their purpose firm and put their trust in you. " Isaiah 26:3, …..... Question to Consider : What would my family and friends say is the driving force of my life? What do I want it to be ?.

Just under this my sister wrote : " My life before was driven by Resentment, Anger and Grief, these things that I'd sought to feel and express, as my reaction to things I'd done or things I thought had been done to me by others. Today, my life shall be driven by God, for his Purpose and his alone, for in this, I will find true life and meaning. For in this, I will find love and fulfillment. 02 / 21 / 2005.

Reading on again to day 6, page 47, " Life Is a Temporary Assignment, " I read to the end of this day, to page 52, where it said Day Six, " Thinking About My Purpose " …….. Point to Ponder : This world is not my home…….. Verse to Remember : " So we fix our eyes not on what is seen, but on what is unseen. For what is seen is temporary, but what is unseen is eternal." 2 Corinthians 4:18. …….. Question to Consider : How should the fact that life on Earth is just a temporary assignment change the way I am living right now. ?

Again just under this she wrote :   " I will worry less about material things and focus temporarily here on earth. I am just a visitor and soon I will go home." And then I added, " ……..And So She Did, in a very bad accident, on July 27,2005, at 9:30 a.m., just a few months after she wrote this. I find this very " Strange ".

(note)

On page 19, I wrote that 10 people would die, and they did just as I had written, and my sister was number 9. In page 20, I wrote, that 3 people would live, and they did, just as I had written, but here in page 21, in God's on way, he again told me like he did when I tried to write and save a little girl's life, I needed to leave her alone, as she was in his hands and not in mine, again here so was my sister and I was not to save her " Life " , but I had saved her " Soul " by changing her " Future ".

(note)

Here I have learn that I truly have the Gift to move " Time " and " Change The Future ", and once again it is not to be played with , even God learned that when he sent a flood up on the Earth to destroy all mankind and all his evil ways, all but a chosen few, not even he could stop " Time " once it was set into motion . He had told Adam in the beginning, that he would destroy the world in 5,500 years, but after the flood in 3500 B. C., he learned that it would have been best to have left mankind alone, in hopes that someday, mankind would ask for his forgiveness . He wanted to see then if mankind would ask for forgiveness , so with the chosen few he had left after the flood , he sent mankind out once again to replenish the Earth , but the " Time Limit " he had first set for the earth, was still winding down . To reverse " Time ", he learned that he would have to die in some way to stop what he had set into motion, as he was the creator of all " Time ". So to do this, he created a " Son " through him in 3 B.C., who was to die and would then " Reverse Time ," giving mankind the choice to ask for forgiveness, or mankind would someday destroy itself .

(note)

   In the following two pages, there is a copy of the online Story about the accident that took my sister's life, as it was reported by the newspaper " The Tribune " in Seymour, Indiana, Thursday, July 28, 2005. As strange as the story was that I wrote about her, her accident would be making History in Indiana.

(note)

   I would like to thank, Pastor Rick Warren, for the material used from his book: The Purpose Driven LIFE, used in the Writing of this True Story

By: Will James

THE   PAPER

" Just What Is It, That Watches Over Me " A Guardian Angel or Angels from " Hell ".

Did you ever get the feeling sometimes, that something or someone is watching over you. Going back over my life again, I began seeing and remembering some very strange things. One of the first and most strangest things I remember, was the very day I was born.

It was Thursday, November 8th , 1945 as stated by the Doctor as he was filling out my birth record and was in the middle bed room of my Grandmother's house. The room was dark with very little light and my grandmother was there, helping my mother bring me in to this world. After my arrival, the doctor cut my cord and my grandmother took me and started to clean me up. She told my mother that she had another boy, but this one was not like his brother. She said that a very strange feeling had come over her as soon as she picked me up.

After letting my mother rest for a while, they moved us into the front bedroom, which was well lit from Sunlight coming through the windows. I could see it was a very pretty day outside and was a warm day too. People started coming in to see me and were telling my mother what a pretty baby she had. As time went on my life was normal for a few years. Then at about the age of 5, my older brother and I climbed up to the top of a very large mulberry tree. I went to pick some mulberries and fell off the limb I was sitting on, and started down through the tree thinking I was about to die, when for no reason I landed on the last limb. Something had saved my life. I told my brother, we better not tell our mother, as we would get into real trouble.

About a year later, my family moved to Colorado .While living there, I came close to dying two times. It was there that I first learned, whatever it was that watched over me was not to be messed with. While visiting one of my aunts, I was playing with 2 boys that had been left with my aunt by their mother, who just went off and left them. One of the boys was standing on top of an old storm house and as I walked below him, he dropped a large rock and hit me in the top of my head, breaking the rock in two. They did not take you to the doctor back then, you got better or died .The Thing that was watching over me, began to watch the boys growing up and caused them to become very vile as the years went by and in their teen years, they killed my aunt's husband and would spend the rest of their life in prison.

We moved back to Texas 2 ½ years later, and I was about 9 years old then. One weekend, we went to our family reunion which was being held in a pasture with a creek running through it. It was a hot summer day and everyone was going swimming. As I could not swim, I was just wading in the creek and stepped into a deep hole and went under. Again I was thinking I was going to drown, when once again, The Thing that watches over me, pulled me up and I was able to make it back on to the bank of the creek.

Time went on then and again the years started to go by. In the fall of 1962, I went to stay with my grandmother and go to school in the town where I was born. I was in the 10th grade then and after staying with her for the first 6 weeks of school, I wanted to go back home. After midterm tests were over, I saw that I was going to fail school that year, so in the spring, I quit school and went into the National Guard. I was going through what is called Boot Camp and was picked by my platoon training officer, to be picked on and bullied by him. After 6 weeks of training, I had had about all I could take from him, and was about to go what they call AWOL, when this officer went in to town one Saturday night and had too much to drink, and while on his way back to the base, He ran off the highway and was killed. This was the second time that whatever it was watching over me, saw that my life was not going to be ruined by this person.

After training, I returned home and went to work in Dallas. I came across a Red 1963 Chevrolet Impala with a 409 ci. Engine, that put out 425 horsepower. This car was one of the fastest cars around then. I was going back to Dallas one weekend, and it was raining so hard you could not see the highway, and I was driving 70 and started to pass another car . As I was going around this car, the tires on my car started to hydroplane, and sent my car into a full spin at 70 mph. The rain turned into a wall of water all around the car, and again it looked like my life was at its end. The car went off the highway and up a high embankment, and somehow stayed up right on all 4 wheels and came to a stop without any damage to the car or me.

About 6 months later, I went to see my grandmother. The town where she lived was a small town, where everyone knows everybody and while driving down main street in this town, I ran into some of the boys I had gone to school with. They asked me how fast my car was, and I told them I had won a few races with it. They then told me about a boy in the next town, which had a 1958 Chevrolet with a 348 ci. Engine, and could run a 110 in second gear, and had beat every car in that part of the county. They wanted to see if I could beat him in a race, so we went to that town and found this car and the boy that owned it and he had been drinking all afternoon, but when I ask if he would like to race, he said yes, so we went just outside of town on a straight lane of highway, lined up and take off .We were side by side for a bit, then my car be gain to pull away from him, and I guess it made him mad, so he bump the rear of my car to run me off the highway. But again, The Thing watching over me, sent his car off the highway. I left later going back to Dallas and drank 1 beer myself and was getting very sleepy. I didn't know when I got back to the main highway going back to Dallas, and after driving for I don't know how long, did not know that I had even got on the main highway. Some how I came around to see that I was going straight down the road, and had got to 3rd gear in my 4 speed transmission, and saw I was running 90 mph. Again, why didn't I run off the highway and be killed?

I lost that car back to the bank a few months after that, and after being hit in the side by an old man that had too many wrecks, and me with no insurance. So with no way to get around, I thought I would go fight in the war that was going on at the time , but The Thing watching over me saw to it that it was not to be, and I went to Hawaii to find my cousin . While in Hawaii, I went swimming one day and was carried out to sea, and again it looked like I was about to drown, as I still had never learned how to swim, but when I got ready to die, from nowhere came a wave and carried me back to the beach. I met a lady after that, that lived in the same building as I did, that had a little girl about 5 years old, and we got married. This marriage lasted about 5 years, and was 5 years of Hell for me. We moved back to her home in Nevada and finally broke up and I went back to Texas. Somehow a few years later, I got the feeling that her and her daughter were dead. I took a trip back to Nevada, to see if I could find them , but learned that after I left, she and her daughter had went back to Hawaii, and after her daughter had got in her late teens, had got on drugs, and had killed herself, and 6 months later, her mother had killed herself. The Thing that watches over me, had made life Hell for them, in return for the Hell she had caused me.

After I had left this wife, I went to work for a City in Texas, and it was to be just for a little while, till I could find a better job, but ended up being 22 more years of Hell in my life. I became a supervisor after a few years, and the people that I was put over, once again were making my life a living Hell. Then The Thing that watches over me, started to turn the tables on them. One person had 2 little boys that grew up in their teens and ended up going to prison, and he lost his wife, and was almost killed in a motorcycle accident, two others retired and then soon died, a city manage that made my life Hell; trying to build a park was turn into a living vegetable for the rest of his life .

I had another bad accident while working for this City, one night coming back from a city in Arkansas, I was pulling a oil tanker trailer I had just purchased for the city, and was going through a city in Texas, called Sulphur Springs. They were working on the Interstate Highway there, and had made a temporary ramp crossing over to the service road, so that you could go around their work area. Starting through this ramp, I saw a very large hole in the ramp, that had started out that morning as only a pothole, about a foot across, and only a few inches deep, and was never fixed, had grown to what looked like was about 3 feet wide, and 6 feet long, and about 6 inches to 1 foot deep. The type of truck I was driving was what is called a cab over truck. This type of truck puts its driver setting over the front axle and the left front wheel of the truck. I once hit a small pot hole in the Inter State Highway one time, in the same truck, that was about 1 foot across and 4 to 6 inches deep, almost losing the truck then, and upon seeing this hole, I knew there was no way I was going to make it this time. So I just locked up my brakes, and hit the hole, and the truck jackknifed into a triangle, and went in to the median between the highways, and was pushing up dust and gravel so bad, that I did not know which way I was going, so I let my foot off the brake, and step on the accelerator, to try to drive out of the dust, causing the truck to cross the highway again on the other side, and came to a stop, in a ditch. After coming to a stop, I saw that my door would not open, as the trailer had bent in the cab on my side, jamming the door. That night, The Thing that watches over me, saved me from dying 3 times in that one accident, First, when the trailer jackknifed, one of the dolly feet that holds up the trailer when you unhook it from the truck, went through the left fuel tank, cutting a hole about 8 inches square in the tank, and just below the battery box that is mounted on the tank, and could have caused a fire burning me alive in the truck, and Second, could have sent the truck in to head on traffic, killing me and a lot of other people. Third, a few weeks later, I went back to see in the daylight, just where this accident had happened, and I saw that the truck had stopped just short of coming to rest on a railroad track that has cross country trains running all the time, day and night. I got only a bruise on my arm from this accident, strange huh.

Another person that had tried to beat me to death, one night 40 years earlier, crossed paths with me once again, at another city, that I now work for, lost his life, one day from a heart attack, trying to end a contract with that City.

In another strange story, a long time friend of mine, who was a Dentist, had made me a temporary upper plate, that was to be in place for only 6 months, but due to the cost of a permanent one, which was about $ 1,000 at the time, I had to wait 20 years to save that kind of money. After finally getting it made, I had to have a Gold crown made. He charged me $ 1500, for what I was later told was only $ 35 worth of Gold, and he gave me only 2 weeks to pay the $1500. The Thing that watches over me, turned against him and had him meet and marry a lady, that would later end up taking him for almost all he had, and then about a year and a half later, The Thing then took his life, through a heart attack, for the Hell he caused me.

As you can see what happened to those people, who tried to destroy my life, and the things that happened to me, that could have killed me, will make you wonder, just what is watching over me, and just what is it, that it has in store for me, some time in my life. Somehow, I get the feeling it's not " God ".

From more true Facts in my Strange Life,

By: Will James

THE PAPER

" Was I Born The Son of The Devil or Is It Just Strange Math ",
This Is Strange, But True.

My sister's father was born on 6 – 16 – 16. He was born with the mark of the " Devil " in his birth date. His birth date has told me many things. The number of children my step father will have and did. 1 + 1 taken from the two 16's = 2 when divided in to the 6 will = 3 boys and 2 girls

Now again take the 2, 1's from the two 16's, and add them together, 1 + 1 = 2, I was always told by my mother, that I was the second son, born to this man who I know and could fill was not my true father, but only my stepfather and again take the number 2, and turn over the number 6, so it becomes 9, and then put the two of them together, and you will get the number 29. The number of years, the numbers here, have told me, I was born after this stepfather. Take the number 6, and divide it by the number 2 and it will = 3, then subtract it from 7 , the number of days in a week, it will = 4, the 4th day of the week, Thursday, the true day I was be born on, then take the number 2 again and multiply it by 4 and it will = 8, the number of the day of the month I was born on. When you add the number 29 together, 2 + 9 it will = 11, the 11th month of the year, November.

Some more strange facts here, my sister's father's birthday also for told the number of letters that were to be in my name. In my birth name, of which is " Joseph ", it has " 6 " letters, and in my last name, same as my sister's father's " Willis ", it has " 6 " letters. If you take the two one's from the two 16's, 1+1 = 2, and subtract it from the number 8, in the 8 letters, in my middle name 2 - 8 = 6, you will then get " 6 6 6 ", and if you again take the two one's, from the two 16's, and add them together, 1+1 = 2 and then multiply, 2 x 8, the number of letters in my middle name, it will = 16 , ...6 -16 -16

It was for told to me, that in the Catholic Bible, there were the two dates that Satan had tempted Christ. Of the two dates, the last was on October 14,29 A.D. . As I was always told by my mother that I was born on October 14,1945, as it was to keep my true birth date from the man I knew was not my true father. If you subtract the year 1945, from the year 29 A.D., you will get 1,916 years, which then takes you to the year date: 1916, the year my sister's father was born, and then add the year 29 A.D., to the year 1916, and it will take you to the year 1945, the year I was born. So here I must ask, does the Devil have a plan for me or Is it just more " Strange Math."   (note) Christ spent 40 days and nights in the " Desert ", the first day would have been September 5, 29 A.D.

Now 6 – 16 – 16, also for told the death, of one of my young brothers. Take the two 1's, off of the two 16's, and put them side by side, you will get the " Hour " of his death, the 11th hour, and the day of the " Month ", of his death, the 11th day and the number " 6 ' will give you the month of the year of his death, " June ". Now take one of the 16's, and turn over the 6, and you will have 19, and then take away the 1, from the other 16, and turn over the 6, and add it to the 19, and you will have 199, and then add the lone 6, to it and it becomes 1996, the " Year " of his death. He died, on June 11,1996, at 11 a.m., 6 – 16 – 16

……….

(note)

A few more " Strange Facts ".

Nazis treated " Lefties " quite well. The Evil Nazi Butchers who ran the German Army during World War II, hated Jews, Catholics, Gypsies, Homosexuals, and every Freedom – loving person in the world, but they were highly considerate of " Lefties ". Could the fact that " Hitler " was a " Southpaw " have anything to do with it ?. Nazi leader " Adolf Hitler was " Left Handed ".

In " Puritan Times ", it was considered " Sacrilege " to be born on a " Sunday ", so to keep from having a " Devil Child ," Benjamin Franklin's father had him " Baptized immediately after birth. These are some " Strange Facts ", as printed in the " Weekly World News ".

Here again " Strangely Enough", I was born " Left Handed " and have never been " Baptized ",……… It also was once said, " That Left Handed People ", were children of the " Devil ", How True It Maybe…………

(note)

" 666 The Real Mark of The Beast or Was It "

The " Beast's " real mark devalued to " 616 " = this is from a Web page called " ReligionNewsBlog.com ", Satanists, apocalypse watchers and heavy metal guitarists may have to adjust their demonic numerology after a recently deciphered ancient biblical text revealed that " 666 " is not the fabled " Number of the Beast " after all.

A fragment from the oldest surviving copy of the " New Testament ", dating to the " Third Century, " gives the more mundane " 616 " as the mark of the " Antichrist ". Ellen Aitken, a professor of early Christian history at McGill University, said the discovery appears to spell the end of " 666 " as the " Devil's prime Number " . This is a very nice piece to find, Dr. Aitken said . Scholars have argued for a long time over this, and it now seems that " 616 " was the " Original number of the Beast. "

The tiny fragment of 1,500-year-old papyrus is written in Greek, the original language of the " New Testament ", and contains a key passage from the " Book of Revelation." Where more, conventional versions of the " Bible " give " 666 " as the " The Number of the Beast, " or the " Sign of the Anti- Christ ", whose coming is " Predicted " in the " Book's Apocalyptic Verses ", the older version uses the " Greek letters signifying 616 ". This is a very early confirmation of that number, earlier than any other text we've found of that passage, Dr. Aitken said. " It's probably about 100 years before any other version".

The fragment was part of a hoard of previously illegible manuscripts discovered in an ancient garbage dump outside the Egyptian " City of Oxyrhynchus." Although the papyrus was first excavated in 1895, it was badly discolored and damaged. Classics scholars at " Oxford University ", were only recently able to read it using new advanced imaging techniques.

Elijah Danna, a professor of " Philosophy and Religion " at the " University of Toronto ", said the new number is unlikely to make a dent in the popularity of " 666 ". Otherwise, a lot of sermons would have to be changed and a lot of movies rewritten, he said with a laugh. There's always someone with an active imagination who can put another interpretation on it. It just shows you that when you study something as cryptic and mystic as the " Book of Revelation " there's an almost unlimited number of interpretations.

" The Book " is thought to have been written by the disciple " John " and according to the " King James Bible ", the traditional translation of the passage reads, " Let him that hath understanding count the number of the Beast ", " For it is the number of a " Man ", and his number is Six Hundred, Threescore, and Six. " But Dr. Aitken said that translation was drawn from much later versions of the " New Testament than the fragment found in the" City of Oxyrhynchus. When we're talking about the early biblical texts, we're always talking about copies and they are copies made, at best, 150 to 200 years after " The Original " was written, she said. They can have mistakes in the copying, changes for political or theological reasons, it's like a detective story piecing it all together.

Dr. Aitken said, however, that scholars now believe the " Number " in question has very little to do with the " Devil ". It was actually a complicated " Numerical Riddle " in Greek, meant to represent someone's name she said. " It's a Number Puzzle ", of which the majority of opinions seems to be that it refers to the Roman Emperor " Nero ".

" Revelations " was said to be actually " A Thinly Disguised Political Tract, " with the names of those being criticized, changed to " Numbers ", to protect the " Authors and Early Christians from reprisals." " It's a very political document, " Dr. Aitken said. " It's a critique of the " Politics and Society " of the " Roman Empire ", but it's written in " Coded Language and Riddles ".   6 - 16 - 16........... a very Strange Coincidence or a Sign from The Devil.

By: Will   James

THE PAPER

" Much Like The Devil Himself "

I once read a book about " Satan ". It was about the time, when he walked on the Earth, much like Jesus did. Satan was very effulgent in Mathematics and Engineering, and would travel around the County, building roads, bridges and castles, along with anything else that someone might need to build. They would agree on a price, and the Devil would then set out to building whatever it was. It was said that the Devil could build just about anything you ask of him over night, as the things he builds were built at night, as then he could enlist the help of his Demons.

After his work was completed, he then would go see the owner of whatever it was that he had built, to collect his pay. The owner, if it was a Castle ,or the people of a town, if it was a road or bridge, he had built for them. They would refuse to pay the Devil, and then would throw sticks and stones at him, chasing him away, without his pay.

I found that my life, after spending much of it building things, for a town full of people, like he did, ended just like his, when my work was done, I was cheated. It was hard for me to understand why, when you put your heart and soul into your work, and never ask for anything, that people would find a way to cheat you out of your due. A man once told me that I had become too good at what I do, having no formal education in Engineering, and could most times beat an engineer in building a project, and that makes people afraid of you.

As I could not enlist the help of " Demons ", to build something overnight like Satan did, I could enlist his help, when needed. While working for this city, I had to take over a landfill relocation project, as this city was facing a 3 million dollar fine by the state, because of too many free Spring clean ups, that had put this landfill way over it's permitted grade for height, and the landfill foreman had quit. This project, if done on a regular work schedule, would have taken 3 years to complete, but with the help of Satan, I completed it in 13 ½ months, putting in over 1500 hours in over time, and was only paid regular time for this, losing over $35,000 in overtime pay, and was never even given a thank you for it. After operating it then for about 4 more years, I was told to close it, due to new government regulations. I had a deadline to meet, be finished by the first of October that year, and again with the help of Satan, I finished it 2 weeks under schedule, and at $150,000 under budget, and again was cheated out of overtime pay, and no bonus for saving the city $150,000 in cash on this project.

After closing the landfill, they wanted me to build a new park for them, that would have a small lake, a football field, 4 baseball fields ,a jogging trail, a bridge, a large parking lot, and a new road going into it . Here again, this was a 1 ½ year project, with me having 80 % of the work, and in the beginning had no help I again enlisted the help of Satan, and hired 5 other men, and finished my 80 % of this project in 45 days, and again was paid less than the

24

Dog Catcher, for this project, and 6 months later, was told to just leave, and don't make any noise about it I had spent 23 ½ years working for this city almost 24 – 7 and never asked for anything, but just like the " Devil ," I now hold their souls in my hands, and are mine to do with as I like.

By: Will James

THE PAPER

Oil : Is It The New Black Plague ?. This is Strange, But True.

The " Black Death, " also known as the " Black Plague, " was a devastating pandemic, that first struck Europe, in the mid to late 14th Century (1347) to (1351), killing between a third and two – thirds of Medieval Europe's population. Almost simultaneous epidemics occurred across large portions of Asia and the Middle East.

During the same period indicated, the European outbreak was actually part of a Multi-regional pandemic, that included the Middle Eastern lands, of India and China. The " Black Plague " killed at least 75 million people.

Six Hundred years later, the " Black Plague " has reappeared in a new form, and with just as much devastating effect, as its predecessor " The Black Death ", only now it is not carried by a small rodent, aboard a " Wooden Schooner ", spreading it's devastation around the world, but, by " Pipe Lines ", and goes by the name of " Oil ", or better known in financial circles, as " Black Gold ".

It brought prosperity, and saved lives, in undeveloped countries around the World, while bringing " War and Death ", to other countries, in a growing Global Economy. While Oil, has become the choice of " Fuel ", for industry the World over, it has also become the fuel of choice, for " Terrorism " the World over, providing the needed arms for terrorist, to help Oil, spread the " Black Death ", once again, around the World.

Opec, controlling the flow of Oil, around the world, needs to insure the World that " Oil ", will never become an instrument of " Death ", like its predecessor, " The Black Death ", of the " 14th Century ".

To help insure this, Opec needs to set up a " Super Fund ", from Oil Profits, to find, invest in, and help to develop, new and better Energy Resources, for the Future of all " Mankind ", and by doing so, maybe we can stop " Oil ", from becoming and spreading, a " New Black Plague ".

Strangely enough today, India and China are fast becoming larger players, in the " Global Economy ", alongside the United States, and once again, just like they did in the 14th Century with the " Black Death ", they are helping to fuel the very rapid pace, of " Oil Consumption ", which in turn, will only help to spread the " New Black Plague ", this time around, caused by " Oil ".

By 2007, Oil Consumption, by the larger countries in the Global Economy, will start a " Wildfire ", in the price of oil, sending the price of fuel to unheard of heights around the World. The Black Gold will quickly become the " Black Death ", like the " Black Plague ", of the 14th Century, that I had warned " Opec " about. By the Fall of 2008, Oil's " Black Death ", will have spread greed, for " Money and Power ", through all the World's Financial Markets, causing a meltdown of the Global Economy.

In 2009, this New Black Plague caused by Oil, will spread through and destroy the lives, of millions of people World Wide, and further spread the cause of Terrorism, while fanning the Flames, for Global Warfare.

April 15, 2006

By: Will James

THE PAPER

" The Time Machine "

A man named " H. G. Wells " in 1895, wrote a book called the " The Time Machine ". The story is about a man who builds a " Time Machine ", and travels into the " Future ", a few hundred thousand years, and meets a woman from the " Future ", who was being raised like cattle for food, by some other kind of people or things, and as the story goes, he ended up saving her and her people, and falls in love with her.

They made a remake of this movie a few years ago . The story this time was something much like the first one, but this time, the man was working on building a " Time Machine ", and was going to ask his fiancée to marry him. He is to meet her in a park, where people gather every night, as it was around the turn of the century, the year was 1900. He asked her if she would marry him, and she said yes. He then, after nervously looking through all his pockets for her ring, placed it on her finger, and then he was approached by a man who had been watching them from behind some trees, with a gun in his hand. He asked this couple for all their valuables, and the lady started to put her hand with her new ring on it, behind her back. The thief had seen the lady's friend put the ring on her hand, grabbed her and accidentally killed her, trying to get the ring.

The lady's friend then sets out to work night and day, to finish his " Time Machine ", in hopes of going back in " Time ", and save his fiancée from being killed. Upon arriving in the " Past ", they again meet in the same park, and the lady asks him, where were the " Flowers ", he was going to bring her. He then knowingly what was about to happen with the thief, takes the lady out of the park, and goes down town to buy the flowers. Upon arriving across the street from the flower shop, the man tells the lady to wait there, while he gets the flowers. As he was purchasing the flowers, he heard a loud scream, and then saw a runaway wagon turn over and again kill his fiancée. Later at the Hospital, after hearing of the accident, he tells his best friend that if he was to go back to the " Past " a thousand times, his fiancée would only die in a 1,000 different ways, which now brings me to the point of this story.

In page 21, my sister had told me, she had put in to stay out on the road this time for the whole month, as I said before, she was to stay out for only 14 days, as I had told her, a month was too long a time to stay on the road, without any rest. She had asked me, if I would like her to come in, and I had told her that she was broke, and she said then, that she would go ahead and stay out. I have thought about what I said to her that day, every day of my life, since she was killed.

I wonder now with the gift, of having the ability to move " Time ", " Forward or Backward ", that if I had told her, " Yes, please come home," would she still have been alive today, or would she have been killed on the way home, instead of on her way to deliver that load, and then leaving me, with a lot more regret than I have now, for saying what I said to her, in the first place.

As in the remake of the movie, " The Time Machine ", if it is meant for you to die, there is no power on this Earth that could stop it from happening, or " Is There", and just like the lady in the movie, if I was to change the " Past " a 1,000 times, my sister would only end up dying in a 1,000 different ways, or " Would She ", like the lady in the movie would have. On the other hand, if you go back to Page 20, there really were 3 people that were to die, till I changed their " Future " , and there is only one other person outside of " God ", that could have changed their Future, and that is " Satan ". I am not God nor Satan, but on the other hand, maybe Satan really was my Father, huh.............

By: Will James, her loving brother or was........ I.......Really..?......

THE   PAPER

" Just A Very Strange Coincidence or Maybe History Really Does Repeat It Self. "

Look at what happens to Presidents that get " Elected " in a year ending with a " 0 " .

1840 =	William Henry Harrison	Died =	In Office
1860 =	Abraham Lincoln	Died =	Assassinated
1880 =	James A. Garfield	Died =	Assassinated
1900 =	William McKinley	Died =	Assassinated
1920 =	Warren G. Harding	Died =	In Office
1940 =	Franklin D. Roosevelt	Died =	In Office
1960 =	John F. Kennedy	Died =	Assassinated
1980 =	Ronald Reagan	Lived Through an Attempted Assassination.
2000 =	George W. Bush	" Will He Die In His Last Year Of Office, after an 8 year term " ?.

And just think, he had to fight in " Court " to get Elected in a " 0 " Year # 2000.

Abraham Lincoln,   was elected to Congress in 1846.
John F. Kennedy,   was elected to Congress in 1946, also the year that George W. Bush was born, so he could become " President " in the year " 2000 ".

Abraham Lincoln,   was elected President in 1860
John F. Kennedy,   was elected President in 1960

Both were particularly concerned with civil rights.
Both wives lost their children while living in the " White House ".

Now it gets " Really Strange ".

Lincoln's secretary was named " Kennedy " and Kennedy's secretary was named " Lincoln ".

Both were assassinated by " Southerners ", who then were both succeeded by " Southerners", who were named " Johnson ".

Andrew Johnson, who succeeded " Lincoln ", was born in 1808 and Lyndon Johnson, who succeeded Kennedy, was born in 1908.

John Wilkes Booth, who assassinated " Lincoln," was born in 1839 and Lee Harvey Oswald, who assassinated " Kennedy ", was born in 1939.

Both assassins were known by their three names, and both names are composed of fifteen letters, when added together, will total 30.

Now watch this =

Lincoln was shot, while sitting in a theater named " Ford " and " Kennedy " was shot, while sitting in a car named " Lincoln ", which was made by a company that was also named " Ford ", that had been built it in a " Building ", that was as large as the " Theater ", that was the last stop for a President, that was named " Lincoln ".

Booth and Oswald were then assassinated, before they could be brought to trial.

And finally, as " Fate " would have it, a week before " Lincoln " was shot, he was in a town, named " Monroe, Maryland " and before " Kennedy " was shot, he was a real close friend of a " Movie Star ", named " Marilyn Monroe " and again as " Fate " would have it, she had spent time in the town where he would be shot, " Dallas, Texas ". She had some " Strange Dates " in her life too. She was born in 1926 and died in 1962

(note)

This story was from an Email I once received and was partially rewritten with some more " Strange and True Facts " about these people.

By: Will James

THE PAPER

Changing The Outcome of a Football Game, this is Strange, but True.

A football team, " called the Dallas Cowboys," were 4 – 0 and where to play a team in a Monday night game, " called The Buffalo Bill's ", who was about 1 - 3. This is the headline story under the picture on the front page, of the Dallas Morning News, dated Oct. 9, 2007. It said, " Game 5: Cowboys 25, Bills 24 ". Folk hero Rookie's last – second kick, is the stuff that legends are made of, in a comeback thriller. Cowboy kicker " Nick Folk " celebrated after his 53yard field goal, as time ran out giving Dallas, the victory in Buffalo, on Monday night. The Cowboys 5-0 win, had scored nine points in the final 20 seconds of the game.

The Cowboys were a big favor to win. The Bill's, knowing this, were giving it their all. They made the first touchdown, and the Cowboys saw that they were going to be no push over. The Cowboys lost the ball 2 times in the start of the game, and it looked like they would end up losing this game, as it looked like a game they played a long time ago against Denver. They were about 0 – 4, the Cowboys were about 4 – 0. Denver came up and beat Dallas by a large margin, and this was looking like it was going to be that way again.

I hated to see Dallas lose, as this has been their best start in years, and in a few weeks are to play another top team, " The Green Bay Packers," who on Sunday the day before, was 4 – 0 and had lost their 5th game. If these two teams can keep from losing any more games till they meet on the field, it could be billed as a game bigger than the Super Bowl.

So to help Dallas out a little, I changed the outcome of the game, by the power in what I can write, I wrote, " Dallas is to Win ", by a very small margin, and then went to bed. The next morning, when I got up and read the paper, the Cowboys had tied the Bill's 24 to 24 and had 2 seconds left to play, and had kicked a 53yard Field Goal, but had it called back by Buffalo, claiming they had called a time out. That caused Dallas to have to kick the ball all over again from 53 yards out, and again as Strange luck would have it, The Rookie once again with a very small margin of only 2 seconds left, would again put it right up through the up rights and win the game by a very small margin, of only 1 point, just like I wrote they would.   A true Story.

By: Will James

28

THE PAPER

" The Dead Zone, A Fiction Story or Was It, Really "

" What Was Thought To Be A Fictional Story, Unbeknownst To Its Writer, Mr. Stephen King, Really Was About A Real And True Person, That Had Events In His Life That Was So Much Like The Characters In The Book, It's Un Believable."

In the front of the book, the author wrote a note about the book. It said, " What follows is a work of " Fiction " (note or so he thought). All of the major characters are made up. Because it plays against the historical backdrop of the last decade, the reader may recognize certain actual figures who played the parts in the 1970's. It is my hope that none of these figures has been misrepresented. There is no third congressional district in New Hampshire and no town of Castle Rock in Main. Chuck Chatsworth's reading lesson is drawn from Fire Brain, by Max Brand, originally published by Dodd Mead and Company, Inc."

What you are about to read here is one of the most " Strangest Stories " you will ever read in " The Paper ". In the book " The Dead Zone, " the main character in this story starts out as a little boy whose name is John Smith and is called Johnny by his friends and family. From what I get from reading this book is that John Smith had to be born around the same time as I was, me in 1945 and him about 1947 and would have some of the same letters in our first names, J – O – H, his John and mine Joseph. This will make similarity # 1.

Here again, in the back of this book, there is a page called "About the Author," it said Stephen King grew up in Maine and has lived most of his life there, both in Bangor and in the Portland area. He and his wife, Tabitha, have three children, Naomi, Joe and Owen Philip.

(note)

In the above paragraph, I find it very strange that of the three children of Mr. King's, he would have named one of them Joseph and goes by Joe, the same name of the real person that is in this " True Story. "

The strange events in my life, so much like the ones in the " Book ", started in 1951 when my family moved back to Colorado, as my dad had been stationed there in the Army in World War II. We lived in Denver. This area of the country is very much like the state of Maine in many ways. This is similarity # 2

The little boy in this story was going skating on a frozen pond that day in January of 1953 and was to be living in the same real state of Maine as Mr. King. There were some larger boys playing a game of hockey there and one of the larger boys accidentally hit Johnny knocking him down and causing him to hit his head on the ice leaving him with a large knot on his head. On or about this same time in real life in 1953, my family went up to a small town just outside of Denver called Littleton , to visit my mother's sister. While there, I was playing with two boys that had been left with my aunt as their mother had run off leaving them with her. We were playing out by an old storm house and one of the boys standing on top of it, dropped a large rock hitting me on the top of my head breaking it in two and again a few weeks later while playing on a set of monkey bars at school, I was hanging upside down on the bars by my legs and fell hitting my head once again on the concrete slab under it afterwards causing me to have very bad headaches for the next 3 years. This is similarity # 3

Both the character, John Smith and I being unknown to each other, was starting to develop a very strange " Psychic Gift, " him in the story and me in real life and both at the same time, from the same types of accidents, in the same year 1953, he in the " Book " and me again in real life. Very Strange, but true. This is similarity # 4

In mid-February about a month later, after Johnny had hit his head on the ice, a friend of his by the name of Chuck Spier tried to jump start his car from his old farm truck, causing one of the batteries to explode in his face putting Chuck in the Hospital. The sight of Chuck lying in the hospital bed had shaken Johnny very badly and that night he had dreamed it was him lying there.

From time to time through the years afterwards, Johnny had hunches, he would know what the next record on the radio was going to be before the DJ could play it, that sort of thing, but he never connected these with his accident on the ice as by then, he had forgotten all about it.

Here again like Johnny, I too years later after my accident and in about the same time period it would have been for him, the late 50's and early 60's, I did not pick the next record to be played like he did, but I picked all the Hits and all the records in the Top 10 and just like him I had forgot all about my accident too. This is similarity # 5

Johnny's Psychic ability started to come to light in late October, 1970. Mine started in the middle of November, 1963, which would have been 7 years before his. A lady by the name of Jeane Dixon had a great " Gift of Prophecy." She actually predicted = The assassination of John F. Kennedy, Marilyn Monroe's suicide, and the plane crash of

Senator Edward Kennedy, John Kennedy's brother and many others.

Her predication of President Kennedy's assassination had made news around the world and no one, not even the President, would listen to her. He was going to be assassination in Dallas, Texas on Friday, November 22,1963. It was on the night of November 21,1963, the day before, that my Psychic ability really started coming to light. Mrs. Dixon a few days before had made the statement that she had been seeing a " Black Cloud " hovering over the White House. Then on the night of November 21, I saw what must have been the same " Black Cloud " hovering over Dallas, as what I saw that night and these are the same exact words I used that night to describe what I had seen, " There is a very Black and Evil Sky over Dallas. " There were no Stars, No Moon Light, and No City Sky Light, just a Black Hole in Space. As that was my first really big experience dealing with a " Psychic Gift, " it would be 19 years later before it really would come to me in a big way and then would be another 27 years before I would really understand that I really had a gift and a little of what it was all about. This is similarity # 6

It was late October, 1970 and Johnny was taking Sarah, his girl friend to the Fair. While they were walking down the Midway, they came up on a game called " The Wheel of Fortune ". Johnny was feeling lucky, but was down to $ 1.85. He started to play the game and as luck would have it, he started winning, and kept on winning till he almost broke the man running the game. After winning $ 540 and making the man running the game very mad, he began thinking, it was about time to go home. Johnny left the Fair with Sarah in hand and she was sick from eating a bad hot dog, and walked Sarah back to her apartment. Sarah was hoping Johnny would spend the night with her, but after getting sick, thought it would be best if he went home.

Johnny left then to start his car and found that the battery was dead. He then went back to tell Sarah what had happened and called a cab. When the cab arrived, Johnny asked the cab driver if he could sit up front with him. The cab driver said it would be ok and they went on their way. On the way they had to go up a long hill and as they were going over the top they saw two sets of headlights coming at them. There were two cars racing side by side that night and they ran headlong into the car that was in their lane killing the cab driver and the boy driving the other car and sent Johnny to the Hospital. He lay there in a coma for the next 5 years till one day he woke up. Here again I was in a car race in the summer of 1964, 6 years before Johnny's accident and the boy I was racing had been drinking beer all day, bump the rear of my car to run me off the road after seeing that he was going to lose this race and as the luck of the " Devil " would have it, he ended up wrecking his own car. This is similarity # 7

It was then that Johnny would start to really come into his Psychic ability, it was May 17, 1975. After getting out of the hospital, Johnny helps the police catch a killer, saves some lives, and helps find some lost people the next few years of his life. In the Last days of Johnny's life, he is trying to kill a man by the name of Greg Stillson, who he saw in a vision, who if ever were to be elected President, would start a World War to end all wars. The date now is February, 1980, Johnny would shoot at and miss Mr. Stillson and end up getting killed himself that night. Mr. Stillson would end up never getting elected because of his actions on that same night.

Here again, the character with his Psychic ability in this fictional story, lost his life trying to kill a man, who he had seen in a vision, that would be running for President, while my Psychic ability in real life, really came into being, after seeing a vision about a real President the night before, who would be killed in real life the next day on Nov. 22,1963 This is similarity # 8

Two years later after the death of the character John Smith in this story in 1982, I for some unknown reason, started to write about the death of people, some I knew and some I didn't know. I would write in my mind that they were going to die in a given time and they would die just like I wrote, some by accident, some by suicide, and some by natural causes. It still goes on today as of this writing November 16,2007. This is similarity # 9

Another very strange " Fact " in this story, the character " Greg Stillson " was born in " Tulsa, Oklahoma " around the same time as me in the Book and I was born about a 150 miles southeast of him in Oklahoma, in real Life. This is similarity # 10

This is a very strange Story that happened in my life, that is real for the most part and true.

By: Will James

THE PAPER

" The U. S. S Eldridge, A War Ship Or Was It Really A Ghost Ship "

In World War II, the U.S Navy was trying to find a way to make a ship invisible to the German U-boats. The experiment they were doing was later named " The Philadelphia Experiment ", and after going badly wrong by all accounts, was later denied by the U.S. Navy that it ever happened. My name is Will James, I was born in Salem, Massachusetts in 1920. After I graduated from High School, I went on to college and got a master's degree in Mathematics. As soon as I got out of college, World War II was well on its way. I then got to thinking that if I was to join the Navy, I could see the world, but after my basic training due to my math ability, I was going to be assigned to work on a Top Secret Project. They never really told us just what they were trying to do at the time, but only told us on an as needed basis.

The things I was asked to calculate, made me wonder just what it was, they really were trying to do. In page 10 of The Paper, Strange Fate " Death in Dallas " I wrote, The First - of two " Strange Deaths ", that put a city called " Dallas, Texas " in the headlines around the world, was the death of " President John F. Kennedy ", assassinated on Friday, November 22, 1963.

The Second - was the Death of 7 " Astronauts ", when the " Space Shuttle, Columbia ", just so happened to blow up while returning to Earth, again right over " Dallas, Texas ". On page 18, " Two Worlds of Reality ", I talked about the " Secret of The Grassy Knoll ". The party or parties who had control of the equipment from the U.S.S. Eldridge, were doing an experiment in " Time ", to see if by means of assassination of a World leader, it really would be possible to change the course of " History ". They had learned from the experiment of the Eldridge, that the equipment used in the experiment was working in part by using the bio rhythm of the Earth's Force Fields. This is where they needed the math knowledge I had, in running experiments using these force fields.

By: Will James

THE PAPER

REVELATIONS, The Road To Armageddon

Date : November 15, In The Year Of Our Lord   2008 A.D.V

I am now writing this, as I was a witness to a sign that was sent to me, from who I believe was " God ". The Sign that I received was in the form of a letter, that somehow flashed up on my computer screen a few months ago, out of nowhere.

At the top of the Letter, it said, "This Is From The Catholic Bible ". The back ground of this page was bright Red and covered every inch of the screen, and the lettering was beautifully typed, in bright Black lettering. It said, and this is all I can remember, as being somehow flashed on the screen, I got a feeling it would not be there very long. Thinking that I would not be able to remember much of what it said, I started to look around, for something to write on, what I could of it.

As I could not get to any paper fast enough, I was then thinking that if it really was in the Bible, then I would try to just print it off the screen to save it. When I tried that, it disappeared to never be seen again. This is as much of what I got to read of it, it said, "The first of two dates that Satan tempted Jesus in the Wilderness, was September 5th and the second time was October 14, 29 A.D.". I remember that much of it, as I was born on November 8, 1945.

I can only now try to interrupt the letter from the colors and dates that were in the letter and as much as I can understand from what is written in the "Book of REVELATIONS ". I now truly believe that letter was trying to tell me that there is going to be some kind of " Catastrophic " event going to happen, between the dates of Sept. 5th and Oct.14th , 2009. Not 29 A. D.

Here again on the night of Dec. 6th , 2008, I have somehow, read what I believe to be the word of God, It said, " When The Tribulation Starts, It Will Last For Two Days, There Will Be Large Storms, Lightning, Heavy Rains, Hurricane Force Winds And Earthquakes Unlike Any Known To Man. You Are To Stay In Your Houses And Close Your Doors And Cover Your Windows. Do Not Try To Look Outside Till It Is Over Or You too Will Surely Die. Keep Your Faith In Me And My Word And Ask Forgiveness And You Will Live Through The Tribulation. "

(note)

The dates: Sept. 5th and Oct.14th, 29 A.D. in this message cannot be found in any

31

Catholic Bible or any other Bible or book in this World. As that is the date that Christ spent 40 Days in the Wilderness.

By: Will James

THE PAPER

Is it Fact or Strange Coincidence II

There are to be two men who will come to Power in the United States, who were foretold could be representative of an " Anti Christ ". On page 15 we learn of the First of these two men. Nostradamus named him " Mabus ". We learn by changing the a to an r and add an h this could very well be a man called Mr. Bush. There was evidence that could very well prove this theory. First was in his birth date = 7-6-1946 at 7:26, it showed he was born with the first of the 2 marks of " Satan " " 666 " in his birth date. Second when you add up all the numbers in his birth date = 7,6,19,46,7 and 26 they total 111. Then by multiplying 111 x 6 you again get " 666 ". The 111 tell us that Mr. Bush will be the first of these two men to come to power in the first month 1 which is " January " and the first day which is a 1 and in the first year of the new millennium ending with a 1, the year 2001 or 1 - 1- 01.

The main job of the first Representative could be, to bring a new War to the World and that in turn will cause greed for money that will bring down the World's Financial Markets which again will in turn, bring distrust among the world's population and the world's governments .

The Second of these two men could be a man by the name of " Barack Hussein Obama ". The first clue here is also in his name. His birth name of which is " Barack Hussein Obama " has a total of 18 letters in it. If you divide 18 by 3 it will = 6 which will then make the 3 " 666's " the First mark of " Satan ", the Second clue is in his birth date = 8 – 4 – 1961 at 7:24 p.m.. By dividing the 8th month by 2 will give you 2- 4's then add the birth - day 4 , you will get " 444 " the Second mark of " Satan ". Mr. Obama was marked twice by Satan and could be a man Second in line to be a representative of an " Anti Christ ".

The main job of the second Representative could well be, after the destruction of the World's Population, Governments and Financial Markets by the first representative, is to tell the world that he is going to bring World Peace and Financial Stability back to everyone. He will be telling the World that he is bringing Change and a New World Order to the People. He is to serve for 42 months and then destroy the World so " Satan " can then Rule for a short time before the return of " Christ ".

(note) Bush's birth date = 7 - 6 - 1946 at 7:2 6 p.m. = 666 President # 43

Obama's birth date = 8 - 4 - 1961 at 7:24 p.m. = 444 President # 44

(note)

32

It was once said, " That Left Handed People Were Children Of The Devil, " How True It Maybe. " Mr. Obama was born Left Handed.

By: Will James

THE PAPER

Psychic Energy, Spirits, and " A Vision From The Future "

At my third monthly meeting, December 11, 2008, we were asked to join together on Saturday Dec.13, 08 at 1:00 p.m. to join together our Psychic Energies, to help two other members to close some portals. After the exercise that night, I somehow begin to feel a Spirit that kept moving his arms up and down and it went on for a week. I E-mail Dr. Patricia Demps, our Psychic teacher, asked her how the exercise went on the portals . She said, the Energy was so great and wonderful she would like to try it again some time. (note) What she had experienced on that day was nothing like what she was about to experience in just a few more weeks.

In the third week of December, while playing a game on Pogo, on my computer, I was talking to another player who had asked me what the letters " TLHOTD6 " in my screen name meant. As I started to tell him, my computer looked like it had died. What I mean by that is, that it did not freeze up or lock up, all movement and sound on the screen and in the computer just stopped, somehow, I had just stopped " Time " itself. The color on the screen turned a dull pale color, as that foretold a sign of " Death " to me.

The first thing I said to myself was, someone or a lot of people are going to die very soon. After waiting for about 10 to 15 mins. trying to get the computer to come back up, I then had to turn it off manually and then wait another 5 mins to restart it. When it came back on, it did not reload like they do when you first turn one on, but somehow, I had restarted " Time " with the same exact web page that it had on it before, with the very same exact game and the very same person that I had been talking too. (note) A strange Fact " Computers just don't start up or even restart without reloading from their starting point, but somehow by restarting " Time " , this one did.

The next week, I again wrote an Email to Dr. Patricia about nothing really, but half way through the E-mail I told her, I will say this, I really do have a question to ask you some day, and as it is one of those questions you charge for, and as it is only a $1 question lol, you may want to E-mail the answer back to me someday before I ever tell you what the question is. (note) At the Dec. meeting, I pulled out a business card of mine to ask her something about it and she had started telling me about the card before I had said anything about what was on it. So, I was thinking if she could do that, then she may give me the answer to my question before I ask it. So now you can see why I said that.

The reply she wrote back on this happened to be in Red letters. This color unbeknownst to her, confirmed what I thought when the computer had died , one or more people would be dying very soon.

In her reply to me about asking her a question someday, she said this, " Well, I cannot imagine a question, you would ever think, that I would ever charge you to ask ,".... Not even one dollar. Ever. Don't you know ..... There are no fees associated with friendship and good Spirits. Smile lol, Please ask away.

Here, I have to stop for a few mins., and go to another E-mail where I wrote and asked her, " Did she feel any change in the level of her Psychic Energy after writing what she did in the red letters ". This is part of what she said, " Thank you My Friend, What did you Feel, or think I felt." Whatever you got, or picked up on, may well have been my thoughts at that time.(Bingo...) In that moment, I sure did hope it was Positive..... LOL, BECAUSE I SURE DID MEAN IT........

Now, I have to go back again, and write how she really was thinking it, as this is what I saw and read in her mind, and not what she had written. It said, " WELL....... I ....CANNOT ....IMAGINE ....A QUESTION... THAT YOU WOULD EVER THINK........THAT I WOULD EVER CHARGE........ YOU .....   TO ASK .... NOT EVEN ONE DOLLAR.........EVER..... ....DON'T YOU KNOW......... THERE IS NO FEES ASSOCIATED WITH FRIENDSHIP AND GOOD SPIRITS. SMILE LOL ......" So ....NOW, ...ASK THAT BURNING QUESTION............ FRIEND...... "

As soon as I had finished reading that, it was at that point that both our Psychic Energy Levels on a scale of 1 to 10 and 10 being the highest level had gone all the way to a 20 level. Somehow, it had created a very large " Explosion of Energy ", with a force so great, that it pushed me back in my chair, and I had to cover my face with my hands, as it looked like the glass had blown out of the monitor. The blast Lasted for 3 to 5 seconds. After what looked like dust settling, I then put my hand on the monitor screen to see if it had really blown out.

I then went back to the top of the E-mail 2 more times and reread it all the way back down, as I could not believe what I had just read. By then, it read just like she had written it.

Somehow, daring the blast, the   " Force of the Psychic Energy " somehow opened a window in " Time " and pulled a " Vision From The Future " of " The Fourth Coming of 2 Avalanches " in British Columbia, Canada, right through the Computer and right out of the Monitor, there was also a Spirit walking across the screen in the monitor and a vision of Dr. Patricia sitting at her computer, and me standing right beside her, right after the blast. This vision looked like a negative from an old picture. The Avalanches would be taking the lives of 8 of 11 men snowmobiling in the back country there and the " Spirit " that I felt after doing the Energy Exercise on that Saturday night back in December was the Spirit of one of the men, trapped and buried alive, by the Avalanche that would be dying in the " Future " 2 weeks later, trying to dig out of the snow to save his life. These men died on Sunday, Dec. 28, 2008 and I saw the story about it on the World News the next day.

(note) Before I had ever thought about even writing page 33 and did not even know what was to be in it, page number 33 showed up 3 times in the file list and was located about half way down the list in the same spot every time. After I did write page 33 and then send it to the files, I then closed out and went to the files to take a look at it and after going up and down the list of file pages and not seeing page 33, I then stopped and went to thinking I must look where I had seen it before I ever wrote it. So then, I went half way down the list, and looked right in the center, and there it was.

All a True Story.

By: Will James

THE PAPER

Time Travel Calculations

Looking At My Life Through " Time "

Mathematical   Date   =   Years   A.D.

The Date = Sept. 5th___ Oct. 14, 29 A.D. Christ spent 40 days in the Wilderness

0.00000000	X	29	=	0
1.00000000	X	29	=	29 A.D. Begin The Last 2,000 years *
1.00000001	X	29	=	29.00000029
1.00000051	X	29	=	29.00001479
1.00000551	X	29	=	29.00015979
1.00006551	X	29	=	29.00189979
1.00096551	X	29	=	29.02799979
1.00896551	X	29	=	29.25999979
1.06896551	X	29	=	30.99999979

1.137931034	X	29	=	33 A.D. *

The Date = April 3th, 33 A.D.   The Crucifixion of Christ

Time Span 4 years   *

10.06896551	X	29	=	291.9999998 = 261 years
20.06896551	X	29	=	581.9999998 = 290 years
30.06896551	X	29	=	871.9999998 = 116 years
34.06896551	X	29	=	987.9999998 = 116 years
35.06896551	X	29	=	1017 End of the First 1,000 years *
36.06896551	X	29	=	1046
37.06896551	X	29	=	1075
38.06896551	X	29	=	1104
39.06896551	X	29	=	1133
40.06896551	X	29	=	1162

50.06896551	X	29	=	1452	= 290 years
51.06896551	X	29	=	1481	
51.31034483	X	29	=	1488	Mother Shipton *
51.44827586	X	29	=	1492	Columbus *
51.82758621	X	29	=	1507	Nostradamus *
52.06896551	X	29	=	1510	= 58 years

Back in Time,   1,771 Years
                        +   29   Years is

                        _____

Forward in Time, to The Biorhythm Year,   1800

60.06896551   X   29   =   1742
61.24137931   X   29   =   1776   July 4th, Birth of America *
62.06896551   X   29   =   1800   Biorhythm Point. = 290 years   *
63.06896551   X   29   =   1829
64.06896551   X   29   =   1858
65.06896551   X   29   =   1887   My Grandmother was born.
66.06896551   X   29   =   1916   My Dad was born 6-16-16
67.010141945 X   29   =   1943.294116 = 28 October,1943, time 10:00
a.m. Wednesday, I vanished aboard the USS Eldridge.
67.06896551   X   29   =   1945   I reappeared on Nov. 8th 1945
68.06896551   X   29   =   1974   I married a lady born in 1929 and I turn
29
69.06896551   X   29   =   2003   My baby sister came back into my life.

          The Last of the 29 year Blocks Ended in 2003

69.13793103   X   29   =   2005   My Sister sacrificed her life.
She sacrificed her life to save 4 others + 1 who would have lost his life a few months later.
(note) Her death strangely enough occurred, exactly 40 days to the date Sept. 5th.
Died on July 27. From July 28 to Sept 5th. is exactly 40 days and 4 years from the date
Sept. 5th __ Oct. 14, 2009.

69.27586207   X   29   =   2009   A.D.

The Date = Sept. 5th ____Oct. 14 , 2009 A.D. The Return of Jesus Christ in this 40
days.   Time Span = 4 years *
The hour of his return is known only to him. But, the Bible never said anything about
 man knowing the Date of his return.

The Last Time This Dates Will Ever Appear, after 2,000 Years = Sept.5th__Oct. 14, 29
 and Sept. 5th__Oct. 14, 2009 A.D.
(note) The Act of The Last Supper. Sept. 3th, 2009 at 6:00 p.m.

69.37931034   X   29   =   2012   A.D.   Time Span = 3 years *

The End of Time on The Mayan Calendar, December 21, 2012.
Christ said, " I am the Alpha and the Omega, the Beginning and the End." Now you can
see it by the Dates.

Sept. 5th__ Oct. 14, 29 A.D. The Beginning and Sept. 5th __Oct. 14, 2009 A.D. The End of 2,000 years, and Time as we know it.

By: Will   James

THE PAPER

Time Travel Calculations, Biblical Numerology.

Date :   Sept. 5th ___ Oct. 14th, 0029 A.D. Christ spent 40 days in the Wilderness.

4 YEARS AFTER THE Date : Sept. 5th, 0029, His Life was Sacrificed.

4 YEARS BEFORE THE Date : Sept. 5th, 2009, Her Life was Sacrificed.

July 27th , 2005___ . My Sister Died exactly 40 days to the date, Sept. 5th.

July 27th. __ to __ Sept. 5th   40 Days, of Judgment.

Sept. 5th __ to __ Oct. 14th   40 Days, For The Return.

(note)   Biblical numerology is the study of numbers in the Bible. Two of the most commonly repeated numbers in the Bible are 7 and 40. The number 7 signifies completion or perfection (Genesis 7:2-4; Revelation 1:20). It is often called " God's number " since He is the only One who is perfect and complete (Revelation 4:5;5:1,5-6). The number 3 is also thought to be the number of divine perfection: The Trinity consists of Father, Son, and Holy Spirit.
(note) My Life Path number is 7 . Now I can understand the connection in all of this.

The number 40 is often understood as the " Number of Probation or Trial. " For example: the Israelites wandered for 40 years (Deuteronomy 8:2-5); Moses was on the mount for 40 days (Exodus 24:18); 40 days were involved in the story of Jonah and Nineveh (Jonah 3:4); Jesus was tempted for 40 days (Matthew 4:2); there were 40 days between Jesus resurrection and ascension (Acts 1:3).

The year 2009 divided by 40 = 50.255 x 29 = the year 1456.525 . Add the year 1456 + 525 = the year 1981. The year 1981 + 29 = Strangely enough, will = the year 2010 The Beginning of the " New World ".

Date 5-25-2009

By: Will James

THE PAPER

Major Life Changes, That Will Happen in The Future

Name of Person :   Joseph   Willis

Year Born =   1945

1945 =   +   19
                  _____
year   1964   major life change = will go to Hawaii and spent 8 years learning the construction trade.

1964 =   + 20
                  _____
year   1984   major life change = will receive a major promotion to job Supervisor with the City .

1984 =   + 22
                  _____
year   2006   major life change =   6 months after the Death of my sister in 2005, I will go through a major Back Operation in 2006 and will retire 1 year later in 2007.

2006 =   +   8
                  _____
year   2014   major life change = ? Yet to come. May mean the End of My Life, as my life Path number is :   7 . If you add the year 2014 together = 2 + 0 + 1 + 4, it will =   7.

    (note)

   Using a scale from 1 to 8 with the dividing line of the scale set at 4, and 4 being the lower side of the scale, means that 4 to 1 are good changes coming in life, and on the higher side of the scale, the numbers 5 to 8 means, a very bad change in life is coming.

In the year 2006, it added up to a single number which was 8 . When you add 8 to the year 2006, it takes you to the year " 2014"., which tells me that in 4 years and the number 8 being at the top of the scale, that there is a very, very bad change coming in my life. When you hit a single number at any point in your life, like the number 8 , the number 8 , or any single number like it, that cannot be added together, to make a number like 19 or 22 can. The number 19 added together 1 + 9 will = 10 and 22 added together 2 + 2 will = 4. The number 20 has the zero in it, to the right side of the 2, which means the same in the adding as the 19 and 22 did, it means that life will go on, till you hit a single number like 8, 7, 6, or whatever. The number 8 , came up after 61 years of my life. The Strange Thing here is, when I work the Birth Date of the United States, 1776 , it toke 234 years to hit a single number, the year was 2010, which when added together 2 + 0 +1 + 0 will = 3, which is on the low side of the scale, which makes you wonder what is in store for the United States, as of this writing, we are in the year 2010.

1 – 19 - 2010

By: Will James

THE PAPER

Dates of Major Events, That Will Change America

United States
Year born :   1 7 7 6

$1 + 7 + 7 + 6 =$ $+ 2 1$
                          _____
 next year :   1 7 9 7   = The First Recession be gain between 1797 and 1800. It was called the " Panic of 1797 ", and was cause by the Bank of England.

$1797 =$ $+ 2 4$
                          _____
next year :   1 8 2 1   = A Civil War Called, " The Missouri Compromise ", 1819 – 1821.

$1821 =$ $+ 1 2$
                          _____
next year :   1 8 8 3   = Battle over " The Bank ", Sept. 10,1883, President Jackson declared his intention to remove government deposits from the " Bank of the United States ".

$1833 =$ $+ 1 5$
                          _____
next year   1 8 4 8   = The Mexican – American War, was the first major conflict driven by the idea of " Manifest Destiny ", the belief that American had a God-given right to expand the County's Borders.

$1848 =$ $+ 2 1$
                          _____
next year   1 8 6 9   = On May 10, 1869, the " First Transcontinental Rail Road was Completed.

$1869 =$ $+ 2 4$
                          _____
next year   1 8 9 3   = The Depression of 1 8 9 3, was one of the worst in American History, with the unemployment rate exceeding ten percent for half a decade. The Depression of 1 8 9 3 can be seen as a watershed event in American history.

It was accompanied by violent strikes, the climax of the Populist and free silver political crusades, the creation of a new political balance, the continuing transformation of the country's economy, major changes in national policy, and far-reaching social and intellectual developments.

1 8 9 3

1893 =   + 2 1
                                    ——————
next year   1 9 1 4   =   The Start of World War I and a strange event called " The Christmas Truce of 1 9 1 4 ".

1914 =   + 1 5
                                    ——————
next year   1 9 2 9   =   The largest depression ever in American History, would go down in history as " The Grate Depression , of 1 9 2 9 ". Hundreds of people killed them self after losing all they had in the " Stock Market ".

1929 =   + 2 1
                                    ——————
next year   1 9 5 0   =   The United States just being 5 years out of the Second World War that ended in 1 9 4 5 , would get in to a smaller war, know as the " Korea War ".

1950 =   + 1 5
                                    ——————
next year   1 9 6 5   =   Again, the Untied States, 15 years later would fight yet another War called, the " Vietnam War ".

1965 =   + 2 1
                                    ——————
next year   1 9 8 6   =   The United States would suffer a tragic accident on 1 – 28 - 1 9 8 6, when the Space Shuttle " Challenger " would explode just after liftoff, and on 4 – 14 – 1 9 8 6 , the Untied States launches air strikes against a middle eastern country called " Libya ".

1986 =   + 2 4
                                    ——————
next year   2 0 1 0   =   Wrote 1-25-2010 , What is next for the United States ?. The year 2010 is the only year to date from the year 1776, when added together will = a single number $2 + 0 + 1 + 0 = 3$. The strange thing here is, that it toke 234 years to get to that number. That is a very bad sign.

Up date : 1. On April 20, 2010, 3 months later, a large Deep Water Oil Well drilling Rig exploded, killing 11 workers and began letting about 210,000 gallons of crude oil aday, flow out of the new well and across the Gulf of Mexico, causing what will become, the largest environmental accident in U.S. history. Wrote on May 5, 2010

    (note) On May 20, 2010, on the nightly World News a government spokesman stated that the BP Oil company damaged oil well in the Gulf of Mexico was losing a lot more oil in the ocean that BP Oil had estimated and now was becoming the Largest Environmental Accident in U.S. History, just like I wrote it would in the above Up Date I had wrote on May 5, 2010. Now take a look at the two strange dates : April 20, 2010 - May 20, 2010. Two bad announcements on the same day the 20th of each month.

    2. In late summer of 2010, Large Hurricanes, will cause unheard of devastation across the eastern half of the United States = May 27, 2010

    3. Again by the Fall of 2010, the American Economy will see a lost, far grater than the one in the Fall of 2008. = May 27,2010

2010 =   +   3
_____ =   3 (2 + 1 =) 3 + 3 =   3 3 3 The Number of Christ, who could very well be the new ruler of the New World in 2013.

next year   2 0 1 3
    Strange huh, or is it really.

2013 =   +   6
_____
next year   2 0 1 9   = ?

2019 =   + 1 2
_____
next year   2 0 3 1   = ?

2031 =   +   6

next year   ———

                 2037

1- 25 – 2010

By: Will James

THE PAPER

A Strange Fact : Could Being Left Handed, Make You a Child of " The Devil ".

This is from the Bible, found in " Matthew 25 : 31-34, 41 ".

   The Bible contains about 35 unfavorable references to the " Left Hand ". In the best
known example, in the Gospel of Matthew, Jesus says : When the Son of man shall come
in his glory, and all the holy angels with him, then shall he sit upon the throne of his glory
and before him shall be gathered all nations. And he shall separate them one from another,
as a shepherd divided his sheep from the goats. And he shall set the sheep on his right
hand, but the goats on the left. Then shall the King say unto them on his right hand, "
Come, yet blessed of my Father, inherit the kingdom prepared for you from the foundation
of the World ", Then shall he say also unto them on the left hand, " Depart from me, ye
are cursed, into everlasting fire, prepared for the Devil and his angels ".

(note)

   Is there more evidence to be added to page 23, that what I thought was a Strange Gift,
really was a " Curse ", placed on me by " God "? As I was born " Left Handed ".

By: Will   James

THE PAPER

" A True Story , About Looking Into The Future and a Japanese Spirit "

On a night in the middle of March, 2010, I went online to read my email and while reading down the list that had come in that day, I saw a strange email I thought was from my friend in JAPAN. Back about 5 months ago, I had turned off my internet to try to save a little money. That caused me to lose track of my friends on the internet. When I had it turned back on, I went to another internet server and had some problems relocating my friends.

The strange email that had shown up in the list was in a darker color than the rest of the emails. After seeing what I thought was the sender address was the address of my friend in Japan that I had sent the email to, so I thought I would go to the contact list while I had their address and add it back in the list. When I got back to the email list again, the email had vanished.

Earlier in the day, I got to thinking about adding some pictures to some of the stories in my paper that had been sent to me by email, and had been taken by a man who was there, on the day Pearl Harbor was bombed, December 7th, 1941. The first picture was going to be put with a story about a man who was also there and was a pilot in the Army Air Corps as it was called back then, and later was changed to be called, the Air Force. In this picture there was what I believe to be a Japanese plane bombing the American planes on the ground and what later took place in this email, the pilot of the Japanese plane had to have been killed by anti-gun fire at the same time the picture was snapped trapping his spirit in the photograph.

The original email I thought had been sent to my friend in Japan, had accidentally been sent to the send folder, where it went unnoticed for the next 6 years and then was recognized by this spirit after being released from the photo into my computer after the picture had been placed with the story about the American pilot. This is what the original email said :

Saturday October 16, 2004 3:06 PM

From: " WILL JAMES " tlssttx1@yahoo.com
  To: planning@fx.ciao.jp

   Hi Hiro, hope you are well and your jogging is going well. It is getting a little cold here now but the days are pretty with lots of sunshine. Well the Presidential Election is just 3 weeks away now and I too hope Mr. Kerry gets elected too. So less hope he wins. They say it will be a very close race. If Mr. Bush gets back in, look for the hold world to GO TO HELL IN A HANDBASKET. Take care Hiro love you Joseph….

Now what you are about to read is the strange email as it was written by the Japanese spirit to me:

Saturday October 16, 2004 3:06 PM

From: " WILL JAMES " tlssttx1@yahoo.com
 To: planning@fx.ciao.jp

  It will be close race Mr. Bush gets back in look for the whole world to GO TO HELL IN A HAND BASKET. 2008

  As you can see, I had to read it two times to understand what it was trying to tell me, and as you can also see how it was addressed, it was sent to me, not from me, but with the address sending it to Japan. Three things here, First : is the date and time the original email was to be sent.
Second: is the year 2008, this year was not in the original email.
Third: is when I first saw the year 2008, I thought it was not that old an email, till after it vanished and later for some unknown reason went to the send folder of which had never been before and found the original email and saw the date Saturday, October 16, 2004 3:06 PM , then I realized the date now was March, 2010.

  I then sent an email to my friend Dr. Patricia, telling her what had happened. When she went to read it, the spirit had attached itself to the email with the energy in the internet and travel with the email into her computer and when it was then open, the spirit stopped " Time Itself ", and somehow stopped her computer in " Time," like another spirit did to mine in page 33.

(note)   In 2008, at the end of the second term for Mr. Bush, just like I wrote to my friend in Japan, the world economy came crashing down and people all around the world were laid off work and many killed themselves after losing everything they owned. It's kind of strange how most of the things I write come true, huh?

(note)

In the following page is an original copy of the email that I tried to send to my friend in Japan, but ended up going to the send file Saturday, October 16, 2004 at 3:06 PM .

By: Will James

THE PAPER

Doomed at Birth, a Ship called: " R. M. S. Titanic "

R. M. S. Titanic, is short for : " The Royal Mail Ship TITANIC " . This name was so chosen by J. Bruce Ismail, White Line's managing director, as if to convey a sense of overwhelming size and strength. The Fate of the Titanic came into being, with the birth date of Titanic, in March , 1909. March being the 3rd month in the calendar year gives you the number 3, then when added to the year 1909 , will then give you the year " 1912 ". The year , 1912 then added together 1 + 9 + 1 + 2 = 13, the unlucky number " 13 ", that would sent Titanic to its " Grave ", at the Bottom of The Atlantic Ocean, on the Sunday night, of April 14, one day later after a Saturday night of Grand Parties, on " April 13th, " celebrating Titanic's maiden voyage, but unbeknownst to 1,502 passengers, it would be a celebration of their last night on this Earth.   At this point of this true story, you may wonder how this was possible. Titanic's sister ship " Olympic ", having a collision with another ship, would then set the " Fate " of Titanic into motion in the Future, by causing a change in the date, of Titanic's maiden Voyage, from " March 20th to April 10th " by sending Olympic back to an already overworked shipyard crew, at Harland and Wolff for major repairs, causing a work slowdown for the finishing of " Titanic " and by this delaying of time, would be placing a very large " Iceberg ", in the future path of Titanic, cutting a large hole down the ship's side, that would send what was called " An unSinkable Ship " to the bottom of the sea.

(note)   The point of this true story is to show how by just saying a few words, like I did in page 21 to my sister, changed her Future, by placing a car in the future path of her truck, sending her, to her " Grave ", and here, by changing a number in a date, could change the future, of The World's largest ship at that time, by placing an Iceberg in the future, in its path, sending it, to its " Grave ".

(note) In the short life of this " Doomed " ship, the unlucky number " 13 " showed up 3 times. First, in the year of its maiden voyage,1912 = 1 + 9 + 1 + 2 = " 13 ", Second, was the Saturday night of Grand Parties, April " 13th " and Third, was the number of people that died, 1,5 0 2 =   15 - 2 = " 13 ". Fate marked this ship 3 times with the " Unlucky number " 13 ". Strange math, huh?

By: Will James.

THE PAPER

ACE'S and 8's; The Dead Man's Hand or Was The Devil, Dealing The Cards ?

In the early 1800's, there was a man born by the name of James Butler Hickok. He was born on May 27, 1837, and later in his life, would be known by the name " Wild Bill Hickok ". Wild Bill was well known in the Old West for his skills with a gun and being a professional gambler. He served in the Union Army in the Civil War and went on to drive a stagecoach after the War, at which time he killed a number of outlaws, Indians, and a few other low life that really just needed killing, and then went on to be a U.S. Marshal. In all that I have read about Wild Bill, in all the gun fighting and the time he spent in the Civil War, he was never hurt, till he was almost eaten by a Bear, while asleep on the side of the road one day, due to his stagecoach breaking down.

At the age of 39, he was seldom sober after being fired from his law job, he returned to a life of gambling and while he was back in Deadwood, at a saloon called Sweeney's Silver Dollar, a man by the name of McCall believed that Bill was the man that had killed his brother sometime back, slowly walked up behind Bill and shot him in the back of the head, killing him instantly. The cards Bill was holding were a pair of " Ace's and a pair of 8's ". All the cards were black and the fifth card was always said, no one ever knew what color or card it was.

(note)   To this Day, Bill's hand of cards has become legendary and is known as " The Dead Man's Hand " or maybe after a life of drinking, gambling and killing, maybe, " The Devil Was Dealing The Cards ".

In the second part of this true story, there was a second man, who by the " Luck of The Devil ", was born on May 29,1917, 2 days and 80 years later after the birth of Wild Bill, who didn't spend his life drinking, gambling and killing like Wild Bill did, but his family became very wealthy from the import of Scotch Whisky. This man, much like Wild Bill, would become famous in his own lifetime. Somewhat like Bill did servicing in the Civil War, he serviced in World War II as a captain of a P.T. Boat, that was rammed and sunk by a Japanese destroyer . He saved most of his crew and later after the war, he became a Congressman, then a Senator and went on to become the President of The United States. This man's name was John F. Kennedy, and his birth year " 1917 ", when worked out mathematically, contained the cards of the " The Dead Man's Hand ". By adding the year together 1+ 9 + 1 + 7 it will = 18. In the game of poker, the Ace case counts as 1 or Ace. Now the number 18 converts to = 1 the Ace card and the 8 card. In calculating the year to two numbers, the number 18, came up in each of the 2 times it was calculated after his birth year 1917. This foretold his Strange death and the year he will die.

                    1 9 1 7

    1-9-1-7 =   + 1-8   (A - 8)
              _____
              1 9 3 5
                         Two pair of Aces and 8's .
                    1 9 3 5
      1-9-3-5 =   + 1-8   (A - 8)
              _____
              1 9 5 3

      1-9-5-3 =   + 1 8 --- 8 = 10 + 1953 = 1963 the year he will die.
              _____
              1 9 7 2

      1-9-7-2 =   + 1 9
              _____

President Kennedy was killed by an assassin's bullet, just like the bullet that killed Wild Bill, as strange luck would have it, it hit him in the back of his head. On November 22, 1963

(note)   This page is another example of how numbers can tell the " Future ". Also after writing this page, I too wonder what the fifth and last card really was. To find out, I took a deck of poker cards and pulled out the 2 Black - Aces and the 2 Black - 8 cards and reshuffled the deck two more times, and then cut the deck in half, and then pulled the top card. It was the King of Clubs, of which is also a Black Card, same color as the other 4 in Wild Bill's hand, now you know what the Fifth card really was, as in " Fortune Telling ", the King is a representative of a male person, and the Ace of Spade is a representative of Death to that male person, that draws those two cards in the same hand, like the two that was killed in this story, and is the only card, of two cards, the King of Clubs and the King of Spades it could have been, as the man who was setting across the table from Wild Bill, was holding the King of Spades, as the Devil Was Dealing the Cards, in this game.

(note)   The odds of me drawing that King of Clubs, of which had to be the fifth Black card, was greater odds, than Wild Bill drawing two Black pair, of Aces and 8's, on the other hand, maybe it really was the Devil, that cut the Deck here, as it was only the Devil that really knew what that 5th card, really was.

                                                        By: Will James

THE PAPER

Satan, The Book of REVELATIONS, and The End Times, Fact or Strange Coincidence.

In The Book of Revelations found in the Bible, it is stated that in the " End Times ", there is to be a man who will come to Power as an " Anti Christ " who is to service for 3 and ½ years paving the way for the return of " Satan ", who then is to Rule for a short Time, while starting the " Grate Battle of Armageddon ". So now you may ask, just what makes me think that we may be in the " End Times " ?.

First of all, back in pages 15 and 32, " Is it Fact or Strange Coincidence ", I wrote about a man who " Nostradamus " showed some pretty good Evidence, that a man by the name of " Bush " may well be the forerunner of the " Third Antichrist ". If this could be really true, just when would " Satan " be returning. I too, have wondered the very same thing, till I got to thinking about " Satan's number 6 6 6 ". As his number has 3 - 6's, I wondered if I was to take the 3 and multiple 6 6 6 like this 3 x 6 6 6 = 1,998 or is it the year 1998 ?

That would make the timing just right for him to put the man that " Nostradamus " called " Mabus ", and I learn by changing the a in Mabus to an r and add an h , you have " Mr. Bush ", who would be the first of 2 possibilities, that Satan would see to it, they would come to power as " Presidents ", of the " United States ". More evidence, of his return in 1998, is that 1998 was just 2 years before the next President was to be elected in the year 2001. The date then would read 1 - 1 - 01, then multiplying that by 6 will give you " 6 6 6 ", the mark of " Satan ". Strange Timing, huh.

Two destruction of power by this first President, first by a war and second by destruction of the World Economy, so far, is only the first of many ways that " Satan " will show the World that he has arrived. The second way is to see that a man of color, comes to power in the United States for the first time, in America's History, following the man that " Nostradamus " called " Mabus ".

9 - 11 – 2010

By: Will James

THE PAPER

In The Movie " KNOWING ",

A little school girl wrote a paper about a lot of numbers that foretold events 50 years into " Future " 1959 to 2009. In this page of numbers, It Foretells events 2000 years into the Future, " 33 A.D. to 2013."

(33) 147 276 426 609 822 1023 1137 1293 1473 1698 1950
  6 12 15 12 15 12 6 12 15 15   24 15
  39 159 291 438 624 834 1029 1149 1308 1488* 1722 1965 ** Birth of Mother Shipton.
  12 15 12 15 12 15 12 15 12 21 12 21
  51 174 303 453 636 849 1041 1164 1320 1509 1734 1986
  6 12 6 12 15 21 6 12 6 15 15 24
  57 186 309 465 651 870 1047 1176 1326 1524 1749 2010   **
  12 15 12 15 12 15 12 15 12 12 21 3
  69 201 321 480 663 885 1059 1191 1338 1536 1770   2013   ** End of Time as we know it.
  15 3 6 12 15 21 15 12 15 15 15
  84 204 327 492 678 906 1074 1203 1353 1551 1785
  12 6 12 15 21 15 12 6 12 12 21
  96 210 339 507 699 921 1086 1209 1365 1563* 1806
  15 3 15 12 24 12 15 12 15 15 15
  111 213 354 519 723 933 1101 1221 1380 c1578 1821* page 37, started here.
  3 6 12 15 12 15 3 6 12 21 12
  114 219 366 534 735 948 1104 1227 1392 1599 1833
  6 12 15 12 15 21 6 12 15 24 15
  120 231 381 546 750 969 1110 1239 1407 1623 1848
  3 6 12 15 12 24 3 15 12 12 21
  123 237 393 561 762 993 1113 1254 1419 1635 1869
  6 12 15 12 15 21 6 12 15 15 24
  129 249 408 573 777 1014 1119 1266 1434 1650 1893
  12 15 12 15 21 6 12 15 12 12 21
  141 264 420 588 798 1020 1131 1281 1446 1662 1914
  6 12 6 21 24 3 6 12 15 15 15
  147 276 426 609 822 1023 1137 1293 1461 1677 1929
  12 21 21

1473 1698 1950

(note) The numbers on this page, represents a specific date of a major event, that has or will change the world, forevermore.

There are two dates left : 2010 and 2013. On page 37, you will find a lot of the dates of events here on this page. The dates here were arrived at, by calculating each year starting with the year 33 A.D. the year that Christ died and was not picked at random. In the study of numbers telling the Future, I can tell you here that something is going to happen on a given date to change the World or a person's life. In pages 36 and 37, I proved what I have said here, that numbers can tell the " Future ".

(note)   The strange thing about pages 37 and 43 is that page 37 was calculated starting from the birth year of the United States, 1776 and page 43 was calculated starting from the year that Christ died, 33 A.D. and both pages ended, in the very same year, 2013. Strange huh?

11- 27 - 2010

By: Will James

THE PAPER

Calculating The Date Of The Death, " Of Christ "

This is another look at how numbers can tell the " FUTURE ". In page 9 of The Paper, I wrote " Christ " was born in 3 B. C. and died in 33 A.D. . Now here again, to show how numbers can tell the future, I will show you how to calculate his death from the year he was born. To start this calculation we start with the number 3, the year Christ was born and then add the next number which will be the year 2, then add them together 2 + 3 = 5 which is the next year, then add the last year which was 2 to the year 5, 2 + 5 = 7 which is the next year, then add the last year which was 5 to the year 7, 5 + 7 = 12 which is the next year. Now 12 being a double digit number we can now add it together 1 + 2 = 3, then add it to the 12, 3 + 12 = 15 the next year, then add it together 1 + 5 = 6, then add the 6 to the year 15, 6 + 15 = 21 the next year, then add 21 together, 2 + 1 = 3, then add it to the year 21, 3 + 21 = 24 the next year, then add it together, 2 + 4 = 6, then add it to the year 24, 6 + 24 = 30 the next year, then the year 30 having a 0 in it's double digit number cannot be added together, so it becomes a single digit number 3, so now when we add it to the year 30, 3 + 30 = 33, the year Christ died, as Foretold at his birth by " The Numbers ":

```
  3    B.C.
+ 2  =  5  A.D.

  5 + 2 = 7
+ 7
_____
 12  = 3

+ 3
_____
 15  = 6
+ 6
_____
 21  = 3
+ 3
_____
 24  = 6
+ 6
_____
 30   = 3

+ 3
_____
 33   A.D.  The Year That Christ Died.
```

By: Will   James

THE PAPER

The Past, The Future, And a, 1884 Silver Dollar.

In Pages 37 and 43, I gave you Dates of Major Events that will change America and the World. I calculated the dates when there will be major events, without a doubt, that will change America forevermore. This was done by starting with the birth year of America : 1776, as shown here by adding the numbers in it $1 + 7 + 7 + 6$ it will = 21. Then by adding $1776 + 21$ it will = 1797, the next year of a major event in American History. Then by taking 1797 and adding it together it will = 24, then by adding it to 1797, it will = 1821, the next given date of a major event. If you keep calculating the next year, on and on, it will, strangely enough, end up taking you to the " End of Time Date, 2 0 1 3 ".

In Page 43, I calculated the Dates of Events that have or will change the World and America, 2,000 years into the Future. I started calculating from the year 33 A.D., the year that Christ died, and strangely enough, it too, ended up at the " End of Time Date, 2 0 1 3 " . When I wrote each page, I did not realize that both pages had ended with the same date, 2 0 1 3.

Now to the point of this Story, when I was going to a Psychic Class, I had given some small gifts to my psychic teacher, and now close friend, Dr. Patricia Demps, of which one was a brand new 2006 Silver Dollar. Two years later, I told her that I was giving her a second Silver Dollar with a date on it, 1 8 8 4.

I then told her that, the first silver dollar being new and very bright, that if she would hold it in her hand and look into it, she could see her Future and it would show her that it was going to be as bright as that silver dollar.

With the second silver dollar having the older date of 1 8 8 4, I told her this, this coin is about 1 2 7 years old, and the years and hard times of the " Past, " had darkened the heart of this coin. If she was to hold it in her hand, and look into it, she could see her past, but not all her past would be dark, as for like the years that had taken a toll on this coin's brightness, she could still see the shine that was left in it and that was to always tell her, that all the hard times that this coin and her life has seen, they will always be bright spots to remember in their Past..

There is one very strange thing about this coin from the " Past ", when you calculate it's date 1 8 8 4, it can only show you one thing from the " Future ", the date of the " End of Time " as we know it, 2 0 1 3 . Strange huh?

$$
\begin{array}{r}
1\,8\,8\,4 \\
1 + 8 + 8 + 4 = \quad + 2\,1 \\
\hline
1\,9\,0\,5 \\
1\,9\,0\,5 = \quad + 1\,5 \\
\hline
1\,9\,2\,0
\end{array}
$$

$$1920 = + 12$$
$$\overline{1932}$$
$$1932 = + 15$$
$$\overline{1947}$$
$$1 + 9 + 4 + 7 = + 21$$
$$\overline{1968}$$
$$1968 = + 24$$
$$\overline{1992}$$
$$1992 = + 21$$
$$\overline{2013}$$

2013   The End of Time Date, of The World, As We Know It.

(note)

This coin, page 37 and page 43, prove that the Date 2013 and not 2012 is the real " Date " of the End of Time, as we know it.

2 – 6 - 2011

By: Will James

THE PAPER

" WHEN Time Began By Math "

God first set " Time " for the World at 5500 years and then it was to wind down to the end of it, at the number " 0 ". What I am about to show you here, is the count down by math, the way God did it.

Years are in B. C., Time :

```
5500  5292  5103  4905  4664  4419
 10    18     9    18    18    18
5490  5274  5094  4887  4626  4401
 18    18    18    27 *  18     9
5472  5256  5086  4860  4608  4392
 18    18    19    18    18    18
5454  5238  5067  4842  4590  4374
 18    18    18    18    18    18
5436  5220  5049  4824  4572  4356
 18     9    18    18    18    18
5418  5211  5031  4806  4554  4338
 18     9     9    18    18    18
5400  5202  5022  4788  4536  4320
  9     9     9    27 *  18     9
5391  5193  5013  4761  4518  4311
 18    18     9    18    18     9
5373  5175  5004  4743  4500  4302
 18    18     9    18     9     9
5355  5157  4995  4725  4491  4293
 18    18    27 *  18    18    18
5337  5139  4968  4707  4473  4275
 18    18    27 *  18    18    18
5319  5121  4941  4689  4455  4257
 18     9    18    27 *  18    18
5301  5112  4923  4662  4437  4239
  9     9    18    18    18    18
5292  5103  4905  4644  4419  4221
```

46

```
4221  4041  3807  3555  3339  3159
  9     9    18    18    18    18
4212  4032  3789  3537  3321  3141
  9     9    27 *  18     9     9
4203  4023  3762  3519  3312  3132
  9     9    18    18     9     9
4194  4014  3744  3501* 3303  3123  ** 3501 was the year of the Great Flood.
 18     9    18     9     9     9  ** 387 years later, was the start of the
4176  4005  3726  3492  3294  3114  ** Mayan Calendar Aug.11, 3114
 18     9    18    18    18     9
4158  3996  3708  3474  3276  3105
 18    27 *  18    18    18     9
4140  3969  3690  3456  3258  3096
  9    27 *  18    18    18    18
4131  3942  3672  3438  3240  3078
  9    18    18    18     9    18
4122  3924  3654  3420  3231  3060
  9    18    18     9     9     9
4113  3906  3636  3411  3222  3051
  9    18    18     9     9     9
4104  3888  3618  3402  3213  3042
  9    27 *  18     9     9     9
4095  3861  3600  3393  3204  3033
 18    18     9    18     9     9
4077  3843  3591  3375  3195  3024
 18    18    18    18    18     9
4059  3825  3573  3357  3177  3015
 18    18    18    18    18     9
4041  3807  3555  3339  3159  3006
```

```
3006  2736  2511  2322  2151  2007
 9    18     9     9     9     9
2997  2718  2502  2313  2142  1998
27    18     9     9     9    27 *
2970  2700  2493  2304  2133  1971
18     9    18     9     9    18
2952  2691  2475  2295  2124  1953
18    18    18    18     9    18
2934  2673  2457  2277  2115  1935
18    18    18    18     9    18
2916  2655  2439  2259  2106  1917
18    18    18    18     9    18
2898  2637  2421  2241  2097  1899
27 *  18     9     9    18    27 *
2871  2619  2412  2232  2079  1872
18    18     9     9    18    18
2853  2601  2403  2223  2061  1854
18     9     9     9     9    18
2835  2592  2394  2214  2052  1836
18    18    18     9     9    18
2817  2574  2376  2205  2043  1818
18    18    18     9     9    18
2799  2556  2358  2196  2034  1800
27 *  18    18    18     9     9
2772  2538  2340  2178  2025  1791
9     18     9    18     9    18
2754  2520  2331  2160  2016  1773
18     9     9     9     9    18
2736  2511  2322  2151  2007  1755
```

1755	1539	1359	1206	1053	837
18	18	18	9	9	18
1737	1521	1341	1197	1044	819
18	9	9	18	9	18
1719	1512	1332	1179	1035	801
18	9	9	18	9	9
1701	1503	1323	1161	1026	792
9	9	9	9	9	18
1692	1494	1314	1152	1017	774
18	18	9	9	9	18
1674	1476	1305	1143	1008	756
18	18	9	9	9	18
1656	1458	1296	1134	999	738
18	18	18	9	27 *	18
1638	1440	1278	1125	972	710
18	9	18	9	18	8
1620	1431	1260	1116	954	702
9	9	9	9	18	9
1611	1422	1251	1107	936	693
9	9	9	9	18	18
1602	1413	1242	1098	900	675
9	9	9	18	9	18
1593	1404	1233	1080	891	657
18	9	9	9	18	18
1575	1395	1224	1071	873	639
18	18	9	9	18	18
1557	1377	1215	1062	855	621
18	18	9	9	18	9
1539	1359	1206	1053	837	612

```
612   432   279   135
 9     9    18     9
603   423   261   126
 9     9     9     9
597   414   252   117
18     9     9     9
576   405   243   108
18     9     9     9
558   396   234    99
18    18     9    18
540   378   225    81
 9    18     9     9
531   360   216    72
 9     9     9     9
522   351   207    63
 9     9     9     9
513   342   198    54
 9     9    18     9
504   333 *180    45
 9     9     9     9
495   324   171    36
18     9     9     9
477   315   162    27
18     9     9     9
459   306   153    18
18     9     9     9
441   297   144     9
 9    18     9     9
432   279   135    O
```

B. C.   Would have been the End of Time that God had first set for the World to End.

4 - 10 - 2011

By: Will James

THE PAPER

Numbers Telling The Future of Three Men, Bush, Obama, and Perry

Date 7 – 1 – 2011   by   Will   James

Bush born in 1946   Obama born in 1961   Perry born in 1950

```
        1946                    1961                    1950
  +       20              +       17              +       15
  _____              _____              _____
        1966                            1978              1965


  +       22              +       25              +       21
  _____              _____              _____
        1988                    2003                    1986
  +       26              +        5              +       24


  _____              _____              _____
        2014                    2008  1 term as          2010  3th term
                                                                 as Gov.
                          +       10   President    +       3
                          _____              _____
                                2018                    2013  Next
```

(note) Mr. Bush was placed into office by the Supreme Court.   +   4 President
It was never written in the Stars that Mr. Bush was to be President.   _____
                                          2017 ReElect.
                                                                      +   2
                                                                      _____
            Perry,   2 years into his second term ?.   2019

47

THE PAPER

2 0 1 3, The End of Time, As We Know. It Date : 9 – 5 - 2011

What is in store for these people and the United States in the year 2 0 1 3 ?

Pauline   David and Nance   Jerry and Donna   Friend's Son   United States   Death
of Christ

| 1929 | 1950 | 1938 --- 1947 | | 2001 | 1776 |

33 A. D.

| + 21 | + 15 | + 21 | + 21 | + 3 | Will add up to the |

Will add up to the

| _____ | _____ | _____ | _____ | _____ | (Year 2 0 1 3) |

(Year 2 0 1 3)

| 1950 | 1965 | 1959 | 1968 | 2004 | |
| + 15 | + 21 | + 24 | + 24 | + 6 | |

| _____ | _____ | _____ | _____ | _____ | Meredith |

| 1965 | 1986 | 1983 | 1992 | 2010 | 1977 |
| + 21 | + 24 | + 21 | + 21 | + 3 | + 24 |

| _____ | _____ | _____ | _____ | _____ | _____ |

| 1986 | 2010 | 2004 | (2 0 1 3) | (2 0 1 3) | 2001 |
| + 24 | + 3 | + 6 | | | + 3 |

| _____ | _____ | _____ | | | _____ |

| 2010 | (2 0 1 3) | 2010 | | | 2004 |
| + 3 | | + 3 | | | + 6 |

| _____ | | _____ | | | _____ |

| (2 0 1 3) | | (2 0 1 3) | | | 2010 |
| | | | | | + 3 |

| | | | | | _____ |

(2 0 1 3)

By: Will   James

THE PAPER

" Another, Door in Time " or " What Really Did Happen......?

Date was Tuesday, Aug. 14, 2012, this morning at work, somewhere between 8:00 a.m. and 9:00 a.m., I was working on my state water reports for the month of July, and I printed out what is called " The Water Consumption Report ", it is sent to me by email from " The North Texas Municipal Water Plant ", in Wylie, Texas. It was the last one of 3 reports they sent me each month. Reading down the list of emails that came in that morning, I finally came to this report. When I open it, there is always a full half page of everybody else's email addresses before you get down to where it says what this email is all about. After looking past this part of the email, something told me to skip over the rest of the email, (My First Mistake) and go on to the file that was sent with it. After doing so, I opened the file and then went ahead and printed it out of the email. After reading the printout copy and making note of the total gallons on it for the month, I then wrote the total down on a legal pad, as it helps me in tracking total gallons for the year. I then placed the printed out copy in the office file cabinet, and then at 11:00 a.m. I took the water department crew to lunch and then went home, not going back to my office, as I only work part time on a 4 hour day.

About 3:30 in the afternoon at my home office, I once again was checking my email and there was an email that had the same report in it that I had printed out that morning between 8:00 and 9:00 a.m. It said in this same report that it was sent to me at 2:52 p.m. I received it at 2:55 p.m. I thought that was strange, I had just printed out that same report this morning and filed it. I then went back over the email list for the day and the email that I had printed out and filed that morning was nowhere to be found, anywhere in the list. So then, I told myself, in the morning, I am going to give my office keys to my wife, and go on to work, so my boss will have to let me in to prove that I had not been back to my office and will show him the copy I had printed out the afternoon before, with the time and date on it that was to my at my home office. I then ask him to call my wife and ask her, if she has my office keys and then ask him, how does he think I could have printed out that same file and filed it in my office if it was never sent till 2:52 p.m. the afternoon before to my home office, and if that same copy is really in the file cabinet and I know it is, it will prove to me that all the things I wrote about in my book really are True and at times, I really can look through time and this time, I got what I saw somehow on paper. After seeing that email with the time 2:55 p.m. in it, it scared the living Hell out of me, all afternoon.

The next morning, Wednesday, Aug. 15, 2012, I decided to keep my keys to my office and go ahead to work (MY SECOND MISTAKE), and around 8:20 a.m. I thought I would just call the North Texas Water Plant and ask the lady that sent out that same report, what time did she send it out. When I got her on the phone and told her what I needed. She replied: Didn't you get the report? I said, " yes, when did you send it, was it before lunch or after lunch yesterday ". She then replied: " I think it was after lunch, let me see ". After looking, she again replied: Yes, it was sent at 2:52 p.m., something wrong ? I then said : " Yes, I somehow printed it out yesterday morning, before you ever sent it ". She then replied: Well, I tried to send it out a few days ago, but my " PC HAD A PROBLEM AND WOULD NOT WORK ". I THEN THANKED HER AND HUNG UP THE PHONE.

A True Story

Aug. 12, 2012

By: Will James

THE PAPER

" Was it Really Wrote in The Stars, or Was it, Just More Strange Math "

Date : Sat. 11 Aug. 2012, The news said tonight that Mitt Romney has picked Paul Ryan to run with him as Vice President. I ran the numbers on both men, and by the numbers, they are looking like a sour bet.

Mitt Romney   born : 1947   Paul Ryan   born : 1970

$$
\begin{array}{r}
1947 \\
+ \quad 21 \\
\hline
1968 \\
+ \quad 24 \\
\hline
1992
\end{array}
$$

Pick to be Vice President

$$
\begin{array}{r}
+ \quad 21 \\
\hline
2013 \quad \text{Next President ?}
\end{array}
$$

$$
\begin{array}{r}
1970 \\
+ \quad 17 \\
\hline
1987 \\
+ \quad 25 \\
\hline
2012
\end{array}
$$

Here you can see the next major change that may be coming in Mitt Romney's Life, Date : 2013, he could be sitting in the office of and as the President of The United States. The next major change in Paul Ryan's life will come in 2012, as he was picked to be Vice President. How lucky can that math be for these two men? These two men were born 23 years apart, yet Fate will change both their lives at the same time. As for Mr. Obama, his next major change in his life, will not come about, till the year 2017, as it was written in the Stars by the numbers, he was only to be, a 1 term President, or on the other hand, if Mr.

Obama was to get reelected, do you think, the events that were written about him on page 32, may very well come to, " Pass " ?.

By: Will James

THE PAPER

" Numbers, A look at LIFE and DEATH "

Taking a second look at the number 29, and the strange part it plays in my life, it told me the age that I will die. To better understand this, I need to show you how this number came into my life. If you take the year my Dad was born, 1916 and subtract the year I was born 1945, it will = 29.

The second time the number 29 came into my life was when I MARRIED MY SECOND WIFE, who was born in the year 1929 and would marry me, aged 29, in the year 1974.

The third time, when I took a look at what I believe to be my true birth date which is 11 – 8 – 1945 and added all those numbers to gather = 1 + 1 + 8 + 1+ 9 + 4 + 5, it will = 29.

To see how 29 may play a part in how long I may live, I took the 3 times the number 29 came into my life, and multiplied it by 3, 29 x 3 = 87, my age at my death.

My wife has the number 29, playing a major role in her life too, first the year she was born, 1929 and second, the number of years old I was, when she married me, 29 years. The third is, if you subtract 29 from her age this year 2016, of which she will be 87 years old, 2016 - 29, it will take you back to the year 1987 or is it the number 87, the age of her death ? .

4 – 10 – 2016

By: Will James

(note)

       29 x 2 = 58 my age passed.

       29 x 3 = 87 my age at DEATH, yet to come.

       29 x 4 = 116 years old of which I will never live to see.

It's kind of Strange knowing when your number will be up…………

THE PAPER

Cards, Numbers, and Death, Hit's Dallas, Texas

The headlines in the Friday morning edition of "THE DALLAS MORNING NEWS " dated July 8, 2016 read " AMBUSH " 11 officers shot, 4 dead. Later in the day, the count was updated to 13 officers shot, 5 dead and one colored civilian Lady badly wounded. The lone gunman, police later learned, was the only shooter, who was so upset over police in two other cities, killing two other Black Men, for what looked like to him, and other citizens was unreasonable force and he was going to kill Police as he had a hatred for all Policemen.

There were some very strange events taking place in this Story, and to tell you how strange cards and numbers play out in this story, I have to take you back in time to the Date of Thursday, June 30, 2016. On the night of June 30, I was sitting at my desk and took out my deck of Playing cards and after shuffling them two times, I cut the deck in half and pulled 3 cards off the top.

The 3 cards were, the Ace of Spades, the 8 of Spades and the Queen of Spades, in that order and are all Black Cards of which represents Death. To pull 3 all black cards in a 3 card hand, means 3 or more deaths will happen very soon. Now here is where numbers really come into play. First the shooting took place, " 7 days later after pulling the 3 card hand, in the 7th Month, and on the 7th Day of the month ", and of the 13 Police that were shot, 5 Died and 8 Lived . The First of the 3 cards being the Ace of Spades, which is the main Death Card in this 3 card hand, was foretelling that Death was Coming, and it just so happened to hit " The Dallas Police Department. ". The Second card being The 8 of Spades , would foretell the number of Police that would end up living, after this deadly shootout. The third card in this hand, being the Black " Queen " of Spades " would foretell the shooting of the one lone Black Lady in this story, but who by the grace of God, was also to live.

Here with the number " 7 " coming in to play in the lives of these 8 policemen 3 times, on the same line in this story, and whereas, Three 7's on the same line in a Slot machine,

means a Lucky win, would you then say, they had a LUCKY WIN, or maybe it was just " The Luck of The Devil " or could it have been, " God " holding them in his Hands ? .

A True Story ………….

7 – 10 – 2016

By: Will   James

THE   PAPER

Is The Devil Really Cutting THE CARDS or Is It, Just DEVIL's Luck ?

Here again, as the Funerals for the 5 Dallas Policemen are still going on, no more than a week later after the Dallas shooting, I once again set down at my desk on the night of July 15, 2016, and got out my deck of playing cards and after shuffling them two more times again, I cut the deck in half and pull the top three cards. They were " The ACE of Spades, The 4 of Clubs, and The 10 of Spades ", once again all Black Cards.

The Ace of Spades is telling me that Death will be on the move once again, then on Monday Morning, July 18, 2016, the head lings of the DALLAS MORNING NEWS read, Grim sequel, on Sunday July 17,2016 alone shooter in Baton Rouge, Louisiana kill 3 more officers and wounded 3. The police were able to kill this gunman which then would bring the death toll to 4 dead in this gun shoot out, and was represented by the 4 of Clubs in this hand and what the 10 of spades represented was, that it would happen just 10 days away from the killing of the 5 Dallas policemen.

I was wondering when I first sat down at my desk, if it really would be possible to shuffle that deck of cards again and pull out a 3 card hand of Death and have the details of the 3 cards come true just like they did in page 52 in the Dallas Killings. Now you and I don't have to wonder any more huh.

A True Story……….

July 18, 2016
By: Will James

THE PAPER

THE NUMBER " 29 "

MY SECOND BIRTH NUMBER OF WHICH IS THE NUMBER 29. IT IS MADE UP OF TWO OTHER NUMBERS WHICH ARE, THE NUMBERS 2 AND 9 WHEN PUT TOGETHER IS THE NUMBER 29. WHEN I LEARN TO STUDY AND READ NUMBERS, I LEARN THEY CAN TELL THE FUTURE.

THIS IS SOME OF WHAT THIS NUMBER TELLS ME, FIRST, MY FATHER WAS BORN IN 1916, THEN STRANGELY ENOUGH, I WAS BORN 29 YEARS AFTER HIM IN 1945. THE NUMBER 2 , TELLS ME THAT I WILL BE THE SECOND SON BORN TO HIM 29 YEARS LATER. THE NUMBER 2 ALSO TOLD ME THAT I WOULD BE MARRIED 2 TIMES IN MY LIFE TIME, STRANGELY ENOUGH AGAIN 29 YEARS LATER IN 1974, TO A LADY, WHO SO HAPPENED, TO BE BORN IN 1929.

IN THE SECOND PART OF THIS STRANGE STORY, I HAD A BABY SISTER WHO WAS BORN IN 1961. I HAD LEFT HOME WHEN SHE WAS ABOUT 2 YEARS OLD, AND HAD ONLY SEEN HER VERY LITTLE THEN, TILL 29 YEARS LATER AFTER MY SECOND MARRIAGE IN 1974, WHEN SHE CAME BACK IN MY LIFE IN A BIG WAY WHICH AGAIN SO HAPPENED TO BE 29 YEARS LATER AGAIN IN THE YEAR 2003. HERE AGAIN THE NUMBER 2 IN THE NUMBER 29, COMES BACK INTO PLAY. IT TOLD ME MY SISTER WILL BE LEAVING ME IN 2 YEARS IN 2005, IN WHICH SHE DID IN A VERY BAD ACCIDENT.

A TRUE STORY

By: Will James

THE PAPER

" Was It Real or Just another " Ghost " Story. "

Across the alley from my house is the home of a former lady named Donna, who has long passed away. She was a good friend of my wife. She was a kind of a little old lady, you call the grandma type, she would come over and talk to my wife most every day as she lived alone after her husband passed away. She had a daughter, who lived in Dallas, at the time and fell on hard times and had to move back home with her mother. Her mother and father had this house built and Donna, her mother, loved this house and kept it spotless while living by herself.

After her daughter moved in, Donna told my wife she spent all her time picking up and cleaning after her. Donna noticed one day how Time was fading away from this once beautiful home and that Time was starting to take a toll on her life too.   As time went on, Donna got sick with cancer and passed away. In the Spring of the next year in the month of April, a very large Storm came through one day. The lightning got so bad it exposed electrical power to all the homes in the area and the rain was so heavy , you could hardly see. I started across my yard to check on Donnas' house and had to stop due to the rain. I looked across the alley at Donna's house and saw a light on in the Garage and the figure of a woman standing in front of a window in the garage door. Knowing that was strange, as there was no electrical power anywhere. No one had been living in the house since Donna's Death.

Since I had a key to the house, after the rain stopped, I went over and went in the house. The house was locked and no one had been there, there was still no electrical power and the light switch in the garage was still turned off. Donna always kept her car parked in the garage and dust had covered it all over. I walked to the back of the car and could see small hand prints in the dust about where I saw the figure standing in front of the window during the storm.

As time went on the house was sold by her daughter to an elderly lady who was handicapped and had no family to help care for her and the house. I became friends with this lady afterwards. This lady did not have anyone to help her care for the house or herself. After about 5 years living there, she had to go into a rest home. I was given a set of keys to the house in case this lady needed help and did a number of times after falling and not being able to get up on her own. After being in the rest home now for about 4 months, she made the decision on what to do with the house. I was asked by her to be at a meeting they were going to have for her with some lawyers.

Knowing the lady had lived in the house and was not able to care for it, I told one of the lawyers, the house was in too bad a shape for her to move back in. She had what looked like junk all over the house and only trails to walk through it. Her bed was covered in old newspapers and old magazines. In one other bed room, the room looked to me like it was stacked wall to wall in boxes of junk, and no way to walk into it. She called me about a week ago asking me to help her get back in the house. After talking to her, I was thinking I better go back into the house for a closer look. I could not believe what I saw. The old newspapers and magazines were gone from the bed, and most of what I thought were boxes of junk in the other bedroom were gone, and there was what looked like a well walked trail from the door into the bedroom, to a closet. Knowing I was about the only one with a key to this house, I had cleaned out the refrigerator a month ago. She had what looked to me like a lot of her garbage. That left me to believe that the spirit of Donna, was still living in this house, and was somehow trying to clean the house like it was when she was alive. The trail from the closet to the door could be what they call a " Portal " from which a Spirit can pass through from one world to the other.

A True Story

1-21 – 2018
By: Will James

THE PAPER

Was It, The Hand of " God " or Was it, " The Dead Man's Hand ".

In this Strange Book, there is a Story about Two men who by the Luck of The Devil, were shot in the back of their head by two different assassins and some 100 years or so apart. In this Story, the First Man in this story so happen to be play a game of Poker in a Saloon and made his first big mistake by sitting at the table with his back to the front door, as it was always said in the Old West, that was something a gambler should never do, as then an assassin can walk up behind him and shoot him. They named the cards the man was holding, The Dead Man's Hand. He was holding a pair of Aces and a pair of 8's, all these cards were Black and the fifth card was face down on the table, and was never turned over, to reveal just what color or which card it was.

Most every night I take my poker cards out, shuffle them 2 times and cut the deck and pull the top 3 cards, but this time I pull 4 and most of the time, I would turn up the Ace of Spades, and this time I did ,which is the Death Card, that tells me that very soon someone, somewhere, is going to die and 90 % of the time, someone or sometimes, it has been a number of people at one time. A large number of these people have BEEN SHOT, a few die by accident and a few by natural causes. You could say that by pulling up the Ace of Spades that I was pulling up the cards, in the dead man's hand.

The Cards this time had a Strange Turn of events in them. The cards were, the Ace of Spades, the Ace of Clubs, the 8 of Spades and the 3 of Clubs which was the fourth black card, but not the other 8 cards. Wondering where I would find the other black 8 card, I went looking through the rest of the deck, then I got to thinking, that whoever was about to die, would be dying by other than a gunshot and by drawing that 3 of clubs told me that the number 3 is God's number in this hand, and 5 min. later it came out on the News, that a lady known by all the world had just died, that Lady was once , A First Lady, by the name of " Barbara Bush," died on April 17, 2018, and the number 3 card being black, meant death by the Hand of God, not a "Gun".

A True Story

4 – 17 - 2018

By: Will   James

~ *Will James* ~

Welcome and we thank you for joining us on this tour through the life and the mind of the Gifted and Talented Genius, Author/ Writer and Philanthropist: Mr. Will James.

Mr. Will James, a Veteran that served his country with the United States National Guard (ARMY), is a pillar in his community [Terrell Texas]. He has made a Multitude of contributions, and is a well known an accomplished member of the Intuitive and Development Team. He has been recognized and Distinguished with countless accolades and awards.

From Humble beginnings in Oklahoma, to the Mathematical Genius in The Great State Of Texas. Mr. James is a Short Story Writer, as well as a Published Author. He enjoys family time with his Grand and Great Grand Children, as well as his Friends. He spends his time working on new and improved mathematical persuasions, Humor and Good Times.

We are sure you will enjoy his style of writing. We look forward to your thoughts, opinions and insight, after you have fully read this phenomenal Work Of Art.

DPD PUBLISHING
Dr. Patricia Demps

" THE PAPER "
STRANGE FACTS
AND
CALCULATIONS

Author: Mr. Will James